They Walked into Darkness

They Walked into Darkness

J. D. Buckingham

**TOP HAT
BOOKS**

Winchester, UK
Washington, USA

First published by Top Hat Books, 2013
Top Hat Books is an imprint of John Hunt Publishing Ltd., Laurel House, Station Approach,
Alresford, Hants, SO24 9JH, UK
office1@jhpbooks.net
www.johnhuntpublishing.com

For distributor details and how to order please visit the 'Ordering' section on our website.

Text copyright: J. D. Buckingham 2012

ISBN: 978 1 78099 700 1

A CIP catalogue record for this book is available from the British Library.

Design: Stuart Davies

Printed and bound by CPI Group (UK) Ltd, Croydon, CR0 4YY

We operate a distinctive and ethical publishing philosophy in all
areas of our business, from our global network of authors to
production and worldwide distribution.

CONTENTS

Dedicated to my family and friends.

Prologue

The steam from the hot stones rose up to the roof of the sweat lodge. Shadows from the fire danced in the warm space. Inside the sacred, man-made tent the four Indians seated there steamed sweetly and gently, smelling Grandfather's Breath as they fasted on sweetgrass and sage.

A vision they needed, for their future. But the boiling stones refused to give any signs. In their trance-like state they could not read any signals that would tell them what to do.

The air was heavy with old sweat, mixed with fear, for they were unsure of their future. The land they lived upon was theirs no more. It had been taken over by the US Government and the Whites.

Any day now, they expected soldiers to come and force them out of their beloved land.

Bared to the waist, Chief Whiteleaf looked serene and impeccable. Inside his stalwart frame, his demeanor was not 'in balance', for he alone anticipated the soldier's arrival. And he knew it would not be good...

An Indian with a hooked nose, sitting to the right of Chief Whiteleaf, stated: "You look worried, Jacob?"

Chief Whiteleaf sighed heavily. "There have been no signs in the fire! I am growing stiff sitting here. We face such a crisis, my friends!"

They all knew to what he referred to; The Treaty of New Echota had crumbled to dust in the Cherokee's eyes. The white man's parliament had won. Their land was being taken from them. Now, they were left to await their fate; probably to be moved to a faraway place that they didn't want to travel to.

Chief Whiteleaf had lived through sixty-seven summers and winters, so he was deemed to be called 'wise' in the eyes of his people. He was the head of a small Cherokee village named

Ahoama. Today, he had called his people from all around the Smokey Mountains, to descend upon Ahoama and hold a council meeting.

In that meeting they would have to decide what they were going to do if the soldiers came to oust them from their homes. For their land had been bought by the White People, because they wanted the gold found there.

They were not fighters. Bloodshed wasn't an option. Chief Whiteleaf's people were churchgoers and farmers. They knew nothing of warfare, for these Cherokee people were not like their ancestors.

They had built this town board by board, nail by nail, and they were proud of it. It nestled amongst the Smokey Mountains, a serene backwoods retreat, filled with wooden homes with gardens. There was a main street that held an ironmongeries store, a stable, and a large two-storied, white-painted wooden building that was the council chambers. It was raised on stone foundations and had a brick built fire place at the end of the room. There was also a schoolhouse, a public house and a church.

Chief Whiteleaf poured more water onto the heat-soaked stones that lay in the middle of the lodge and the four men were engulfed in its misty vapor. He would soon have to get ready to meet his people, and he had had no sign. He was a very disturbed man. He said now: "We have spent long time in here. Soon, now, all our people will join us at the council chambers. We will have to tell them about this present situation."

Another old Indian raised a fist and shook it. "Our people will not like to leave this land. We must fight the soldiers when they come! It would be better to die here than die elsewhere."

Chief Whiteleaf sucked in his fleshy under lip which made his mouth form a straight line of disapproval. He shook his long grey-haired head. "I disagree. While there is life there is hope. They would retaliate and slaughter our families. Look around you at what we have accomplished over the years – our homes, a community!"

The Indian sitting the other side of Chief Whiteleaf, stretched his legs in the cramped space of the lodge: "So you think we should not fight them, Jacob?"

"No! We look after the land and speak with God. We are no longer the savages of old."

Their medicine man, Najun, said: "Jacob speaks true. We no longer shed blood. We Cherokee are now a proud, civilized nation! We shouldn't have to bow to anyone!"

Chief Whiteleaf said: "I'm afraid the soldiers will make us bow to them. They will have weapons. We only have arrows, knives and pitchforks! No. We are truly civilized now – as Najun said – and the Government knows this. They have found easy ways to overcome us with their so-called treaties and rights of land!"

The Indian who'd raised his fist, agreed, but he still persisted upon his own scheme. He spoke dryly: "Yes, we are civilized because we wear western clothes, own a printing press, and send our children to school. But many of our younger blood will want to seek ways to stop the soldiers from taking us from our homes. That is right! That is good!"

Najun spoke heatedly: "They will send too many soldiers. Our young bloods will not be able to fight them all!"

The men fell silent, in despair.

Chief Whiteleaf sighed heavily. He held up his hands. "My friends... Be at peace. If we are to survive, we must be like the Opossum and play dead; we must wait and see what happens to us. We are in the hands of God. Let us go now and leave this lodge. We must counsel our people with strength in our hearts and calmness in our words. I am going to change."

Later, when the elders had left him, Chief Whiteleaf emerged from the sweat lodge wearing his Sunday best clothes. He saw that carriages and open wagons were already pulling up outside the council chambers.

He slowly chewed his tobacco waiting for his people's friendly greetings.

Folk hailed the old chief with pride in their voices. For it was only Chief Whiteleaf and a handful of Elders who remembered the old ways; this was when the Cherokee lived in log and mud huts grouped around the town square, called the Council House, where ceremonial and public meetings were held. The council houses then were seven-sided and represented the seven clans of the Cherokee Indians: Bird, Paint, Deer, Wolf, Blue, Long Hair and Wild Potato. But that was a long time ago, in his youth. Now, the Cherokee people lived in modern wooden homesteads.

Chief Whiteleaf remembered all this. He remembered also, that he was proud of his village. He glanced at his fob watch, spat out the tobacco, and, a little painfully, as his short legs were stiff and sore in the wintertime chill, he ambled over towards the council chambers.

He was young and fit and strong, and he searched for 'something more' in life. That was why Nathan Billings had joined the 7th Infantry under Captain Rufus McGinty. The army world was hard, but the lad was used to toil.

His mother had died of the smallpox when he was six, and he'd been brought up by his gran'pa, his father having left them the day Nathan was born.

He'd lived on a farm ranch, seeing to the animals from dawn to dusk, a hard worker, to the satisfaction of his gran'pa.

But life pulled at him, making him yearn for broader teachings than just calving and feeding chickens and goats. One hot day on the prairie, he'd washed his shoulder-length dark brown hair, combed his sideburns that grew bushy around his square, rustic, suntanned face and put on his best coat and leggings, which were a bit tight on his solid, growing frame. Then he went and sat down for breakfast.

After finishing his breakfast of bread and a fat slice of bacon, he began to say what was on his mind. "Gran'pa... Ah'm eighteen years old today—"

Through sun-slit eyes his gran'pa nodded his head. "So you be! Well, I'm danged, Boy—"

"An' ah want to leave home."

The older man leaned back in his chair, holding a steaming cup of coffee halfway to his lips. "Well – dang me!" he repeated in amazement. "You're going to leave me, then?"

"That's right, Gran'pa. Ah've been thinking about this for a long time."

"You hanker for adventure, eh?" Nathan's gran'pa scratched his bald head. "Well, Ah understand, boy! Ah'm right sorry you want to go, but ah can't keep you here against your will!"

"Thanks, Gran'pa. Ah knew you'd understand!"

"Sure, but Ah'll miss you! Where the hell are you going to?"

Nathan told him; he was going to join the army.

Now, two years later, under McGinty, Nathan became a soldier, trained in physical combat. He'd travelled widely, lying with his head on his saddle, under the warm stars, listening to the soldier's stories of excursions and battles won. He'd learned to shoot and hold order. And he'd learned how to kill. Not that that part was ever easy for him to come to terms with. He was a carefree countryman at heart, who loved nature and everything and everyone around him. He brought these traits to the army and found himself quite popular – especially with the women, while the men admired his honesty.

Now he rode with his fellow soldiers towards Ahoamah, ready to obey orders and to endure whatever it took to act like a man.

Chapter One

The Roundup

The soldiers came to Ahoama that very day, just as Chief Whiteleaf dreaded, when all were at the council meeting. It was cold, and the hard ground glittered under a layer of frost.

They surrounded Ahoama, stopping in disorderly array alongside the white painted council building with its open blue shutters. This wide open-spaced street was already chock-full with wagons, carriages and horses tethered to railings. All the Cherokee people who lived in the district were attending the meeting.

The soldiers carried rifles and bayonets, their faces grim and unfriendly as they swarmed the council headquarters.

The mass of them poured into the meeting room, firing their rifles. Several Indians fell, dead, and women screamed.

The soldier's mud-stained caped uniforms and high, round hats with monograms emblazoned on the front, their white frozen faces sprouting rugged beards, made fifteen-year-old Ellie shriek in fear when she heard the guns go off and saw men fall to the ground.

She had been standing at the back of the hall with her mother, Alison. They both shrunk back against the whitewashed wall, horrified to see their townsfolk being threatened with rifles and bayonets. There was the smell of blood and gun powder in the air.

A soldier appeared beside them. He was ginger-haired with a drooping moustache, and he wore a hat. He pointed a rifle at them.

"Move!"

Before either could speak he was pushing them with the tip of his bayonet.

Alison found her voice and said to the soldier: "Don't you dare point that rifle at me, you beast!"

The soldier didn't understand her very well, he just answered: "Move, Indian! Ah won't tell ye again! Over there – where the others are!"

Alison tried to protest again but her words were lost as she and Ellie stumbled to where he ordered, her dark Indian eyes noting the complete chaos around her. Soldiers everywhere, rounding up her people, including Chief Whiteleaf, who was also Ellie's grandfather.

Ellie stomped along behind her mother, thoroughly frightened at the violence and the menacing nearness of the soldier's weapons. She expected a blow to come her way any minute. She saw other soldiers mingling with the Indians, pushing and prodding, and clubbing those with their rifle butts who wouldn't obey their orders.

"Come on – over there! That way, Ah said!"

"Pick that woman up. Put her with the rest—"

"Leave her – she's my wife, she's fainted!"

"Don't argue! Pick her up or I'll shoot her!"

"Why – you son of a bitch!"

The Indian lurched at the soldier. The armed man simply stepped back and swiped the Indian on the head with the butt of his rifle. The man went down beside his wife. They were both dragged away by more soldiers.

Guards were being stationed at strategic points, keeping the Indians and some of their black slaves massed together in a tight knot of fear in the middle of the assembly room.

"What is going on?" Alison demanded, breathlessly, having reached the crowd of Indians that the soldier was pushing them towards. She pulled Ellie tightly to her.

The Indian standing to her right, quickly answered. "The Government has betrayed us! Remember the treaty? The Whites have our land. They've been threatening to move us out for a long time now. But we were the ones who refused to go! I've heard rumors that they might invade. Now they've come to take us away!"

Alison glared at the Indian. "I heard the rumors too, but it's an outrage! They can't do this to us! We were told we could stay here for as long as there was hunting in the valley and water trickling from our streams! This is the land of our fathers. It's sacred!"

The Cherokee, an affluent Indian in his own right, dressed in a smart blanket coat against the cold and wearing a red sash turban around his forehead, shrugged, his eyes darting narrowly here and there, watching the soldiers warily, as were those grouped around them.

Ellie, her heart still thumping, keeping close to her mother, also glanced around, recognizing her seventeen-year-old cousin, Jobe. He was short for his age, and worked in the stables, looking after the horses. But he wasn't looking at her; he was glaring hard at the guards surrounding them, his fists clenched, wanting to fight the soldiers. Beside him, his sister Nancy was clinging to her frightened mother, Rachel. They were staring at the Indian lying, dead, at their feet.

He was a man whom they knew.

Chapter Two

Indian Exodus

The outraged shouting and the cries had died down. The soldiers stood back, smug and victorious now they had the Indians penned like sheep in their own council chambers. The dead lay haphazardly on the floor. Women sobbed helplessly, comforted by their relatives.

Suspicion and disquiet hung about the room.

From out of the dark ring of silent soldiers, a man with long, fair hair, a yellow trimmed beard and no hat came striding towards them.

"Mama, look at the tall man!" Ellie had never seen a white man so high; he looked at least six-foot-four.

Chief Whiteleaf, in his two-piece dark suit, white trade shirt, and colored waistcoat, stood with his arms folded and his short booted polished legs astride, his chin held up proudly as the white man in uniform approached him. His heart beat uncomfortably and his chest hurt, but he gave no outward sign of his inner turmoil.

The tall stranger gave no salute. His face was long and sharp and he spoke to the old chief in the clipped tone of one who commanded authority.

"Your Chief Whiteleaf, aren't you? As of now your folks are under military arrest! By order of the Government we're moving you all out. You're to follow my men to a new place – a new camp! We're going now so there is no time to collect your belongings."

The Chief's grey-haired wife, Martha, Ellie's grandmother, hovered impassively beside Chief Whiteleaf, a heavily-colored shawl around her shoulders, her round face thrust foreword pugnaciously. She was a large, buxom woman with bright and shrewd berry-brown eyes. She kept an impassive council, waiting for her husband to speak first.

Chief Whiteleaf remained with his arms folded. "There was rumor that you would come, but to attack us like this! Who are you that we follow such orders?"

Sharp green hooded eyes surveyed the old Indian. "Captain Rufus McGinty, 7th Infantry."

"We are not ready to go. Where are you taking us?"

"You'll be told. Tell your people to move – now!"

Martha planted herself in front of her husband. "You arrive on our land and order us to leave! This is our home!"

The same green, sharp and penetrating eyes surveyed her coldly. "It isn't any longer. Plans have been in operation since the treaty to oust all Indians outa here – you know 'bout that. Haven't you noticed our army wagons driving along the track? We've been picking your lot up from all over the county as way back as May time. Now it's your turn, so get movin'!"

Haughtily, the tall captain turned on his heel and began to walk away.

Outside, more menace was in the air, as windows smashed and horses neighed in panic. Ellie suddenly swung away from her mother: "Look – out there! They are taking my horse, Mama!" Her pony, Agali, meaning 'sun is shining', was being meekly led away by one of the soldiers.

The alarmed girl made to rush out of the council hall, regardless of the soldier with the bayonet aimed at them. Her mother held her back, roughly.

"Stay here!" she hissed through set teeth, mouth gummed together in dread and horror.

"But – it's Agali!"

"We cannot help him now, Ellie. See? They are taking all our horses! They are taking everything! There isn't much we can do!"

Ellie stared up at the anguish and anger in her mother's voice, as Alison frowned at her beautiful two-story town house with its wide verandah and rocking chair, which was opposite the council building. Its wooden structure had recently been given a fresh coat of whitewash. It had looked neat and tidy in the cold air. Now its windows were smashed and its clapboard front door was open to the elements. White people who had followed the men in uniform were running in and out of it, carrying what spoils they could.

Ellie was still set to go and rescue her beloved pony. Mutinously, when Alison pulled her closer to her, the girl stood her ground.

"Drat them – I shan't let them take him!"

"Come – we'll be moving soon. I don't like it either, but we have no choice!"

Ellie wrested herself from her mother's grip and stamped over to McGinty, her awe and fear forgotten in her indignation at the taking away of her beloved pony.

When she reached him she shouted up at him: "I want my horse back, Tall Man!"

Six-foot four inches of lean, taut male glowered down at Ellie's five-foot-six. McGinty saw a dimpled, round face, with huge flashing brown, angry eyes. She had a maze of darkly burnished hair, combed through with bear grease to make it shine. Her rosebud mouth quivered. The girl wore a deerskin fawn-colored shift dress down to the thigh, belted at the waist with a blue hand-painted, hand-made belt. The dress was fastened at the neck by a decorated pin made of bone. A woven red underskirt made of wild hemp had long fringes on it that fluttered down her legs. She wore soft leather moccasins that were laced to the knee and decorated with colored seed beads. They were in her pierced ears as well. Around her slim shoulders was draped a colored, Indian patterned shawl, and around her neck was tied a jaunty red hemp scarf. She was quite a looker, he acknowledged to himself.

He was busy, but she drew his interest. He asked: "What's

your name, gal?"

Ellie drew herself up to her full height. "My name is Ellie Sheldon Starr!"

McGinty creased his eyes but it wasn't a smile. "Well, Ellie Sheldon Starr. We're commissioning all the livestock – for *your* information!"

"You're *stealing* them!"

"Ah, one minute, you're living under *my* law now, missy. Those horses belong to the army – as well as everything else!"

Ellie obstinately shook her head. "You're purloining and thievin' from us!"

The light of battle was in her eyes, but McGinty wasn't having any of it. He took a deep breath. "Ah've explained. These ain't normal times – so – move back to where you came from and get into line!"

What induced her to stand her ground Ellie didn't know. "I will not, Tall Man!"

Alison had advanced to be near her daughter, now she hissed warningly: "Ellie!"

McGinty puffed out his narrow chest and raised his hand. Ellie stepped back a little, thinking he was going to hit her. McGinty merely wagged a finger at her. "Quite pig-headed aren't you, miss? Ah will not tolerate this attitude from a slip o' a gal!"

"Pig – oh, you mean stubborn! So I might be, but I want my horse back!" Ellie repeated loudly, and, greatly daring, she tugged at McGinty's arm, to Alison's horror.

He shook her hand off his arm as if it was a baleful snake and bellowed: "Sergeant Mallows!"

"Yes, sir!" A burly soldier marched towards them, his face as round as his stomach.

McGinty waved an indifferent arm towards Ellie and Alison. "Remove these women, Sergeant!"

"Aye, sir!"

Mallows huge, meaty hands fastened on Ellie and Alison's

arms and the pair were frog-marched towards where Chief Whiteleaf stood. Mallows grip was strong and he wasn't having any nonsense.

McGinty turned away from them, dismissing Ellie and her mother from his mind as if he was flicking a troublesome fly off of his coat.

Alison's lips were tight. She grunted: "You shouldn't have done that, Ellie. He might have harmed you!"

"I had to do something, Mama! Their doing what they like to our homes and property. It isn't fair!"

Alison glanced unhappily around her. She shivered, and it wasn't because of the cold. "They smashed our front windows," she said, mournfully, remembering her warm home. A tear wound down her narrow cheek.

Ellie immediately hugged her mother. "Are we really leaving Ahoama, Mama? But I've lived here all my life!"

Alison looked over at Chief Whiteleaf who was deep in talk with some of the men of the village. She nodded dolefully. "I know, honey. It's true. I can hardly bear it – let alone believe it! We really are saying goodbye to our precious homes.. But I never expected we would go like this!" She glanced at Ellie in sorrow. "I'm sorry, Ellie. I promised your Pa on his dying day that I'd look after you, but I'm not so sure that I can keep that promise now!"

"What do you mean, Mama?"

"I mean that if we ever get separated when we march, I can't keep an eye on you!"

Ellie hugged her again: "I promise I'll stay close to you!"

"You must! Don't go off like you did just now.?"

"Alright. I promise that I won't leave you, Mama.."

Ellie said this to please her mother, but all she wanted to do was fight the soldiers who'd stormed into her life and who were changing it this day, she sensed, beyond recognition.

Chief Whiteleaf came up to them. "Ellie, leave the talking to me! Don't interfere! The yellow-haired one will not brook any arguments!"

"But look what they are doing to our properties!"

Chief Whiteleaf sighed. His large, deeply lined but humorous face looked haggard and drawn, and he still massaged his chest where the pain hadn't quite gone. "I know; it is hard to see our properties being desecrated like this. But we must accept what is happening. We will have a new home to go to – a new beginning. Be brave, little one! And you, my daughter, keep faith with the tribe!" He put his hand on Alison's bony shoulder. Alison could only nod. Her throat was tight with unshed tears. She was too proud to cry. She took her example from Chief Whiteleaf and held her head high.

She said: "We are Cherokee. We should fear nothing!"

"That's my daughter!" Chief Whiteleaf shook her shoulder warmly. He ruffled Ellie's burnished hair.

He said, firmly, as if to remind them again: "We will have a home at the end of this. In the meantime, we must survive the best way we can."

Martha had been talking with the women. She now came up to Chief Whiteleaf, clasping her shawl. She was cold, but she wouldn't allow herself to show it. She was as determined as Chief Whiteleaf to hide her dismay at this turn of events.

She'd heard the end of Chief Whiteleaf's speech. "We will survive, my husband! We will stand together – all of us!"

Chief Whiteleaf kissed her on her wrinkled cheek. "You speak well! We will be forced to move shortly, I guess, so try and stay together. In solidarity is our strength!"

McGinty returned to them and slunk up to Chief Whiteleaf like a panther on the prowl. He spoke disdainfully, as if he couldn't give a damn what happened to the Indians: "My order's is to take everyone here… Those who've got horses left, saddle up. Those who haven't, follow the oxen and the Government wagons! Those who don't obey the order will be shot."

Ellie looked up at her mother, her eyes questioning, but Alison could give her daughter no reassurance, her worried eyes were full of foreboding. They were fastened on the half-blood Christian preacher man who lived in their village, Frank. He was shaking his grey head, not looking at her.

There was no time to go and fetch anything; they were both shoved and jostled as the Indians around them were prodded forward by the rifles. The little children waved their tiny hands to Ahoama, trying to catch a last glimpse of their home. Many cried for their toys as they said their sad farewells. The men were not ashamed to cry either.

Some of the Cherokees's wanted to pick up their belongings. Anger broke out as they tried to break out of the crude circle they were hemmed into, and were threatened with a bullet in their throat.

"But I haven't got a coat!" One Cherokee woman wailed.

"Ye'll be given stuff – blankets, food, on the journey," she was told.

Outside now, Chief Whiteleaf had worked his way to the front of the queue following McGinty. Ignoring the rifles pointed at him he shouted to the tall, blond-haired captain: "We cannot just leave. What about our carriages? What about our dead? They must be buried with honor!"

"There's no time for that! Cholera won't follow us now that it's wintertime!"

For answer, Chief Whiteleaf signaled to one of the crying woman who came forward and stood by his side instantly, her eyes red with weeping, wringing her hands in a beseeching gesture.

"This woman has lost her man! He was well-known to us; you must allow us the time for a decent burial!"

McGinty's sharp green eyes swept over the woman. He shook his head and the cold wind stirred his long hair. "You can't do what you want anymore, Injun. No more religious ceremonies.

We go now. Ah'll leave a platoon here to bury the dead. That's my offer – take it or leave it!"

"Then our ancestors shall hear this injustice and they will cry on the winds! We cannot leave our sacred land and our people to rot like this! The women cannot mourn their men if they are left in this way! It's sacrilege!"

There were murmurs of assent.

McGinty looked grimly down on Chief Whiteleaf. "Ah've said before; it isn't your land – it's the Government's now! If you refuse to go Ah'll have you all mown down where you stand. Do you hanker for more bloodshed? Ah could shoot you all like the dogs that you are!"

At his words, several soldiers around the captain took a stance and cocked their rifles, aiming at the old chief.

Chief Whiteleaf slowly looked around him, at the scared Indian faces near him, then at the unfriendly soldiers standing with their weapons ready.

His silence spoke volumes as he put his arm heavily around his wife, and he turned his back on the captain.

As if this was a sign to his disbelieving people the large knot of men and women seemed to snap into separate pieces as if a taut elastic band had suddenly broken; they straightened into line sullenly allowing defeat, their head's downcast, as they formed a human chain. The uncaring soldiers framed them on either side, watching. In their rebellious eyes was a death wish placed on every Indian there.

The Indians sensed their dangerous, unquiet menace. The soldier's seemed to blow hate at them beyond comprehension…

They began to move as ordered, suddenly prisoners. Men, woman and children shuffling forward, downcast, dejected and fuming in turn at those who had erupted into their quiet, natural surroundings and disrupted their way of life.

For those left in the big assembly room of the council chambers it mirrored all their emotions as they left it for good.

They were being jerked from the Smoky Mountains and green valleys of their homeland, never to see it again. It was heart-breaking for the proud Cherokees.

As they left in subdued misery and frustrated anger, they could see the soldier's fresh plunder of their beloved village. Other Whites from various different communities who had drawn up to watch the proceedings were also taking things.

Chapter Three

Starting Out

Ellie was tired. Her mother was tired. They were both cold, their breath billowing in an icy cloud from their mouths even though they were wearing course blankets over their best clothes, handed out to them by the surly soldiers. They'd been walking all day, following some of the provision wagons with just two sorry stops to eat cornbread and roasted green corn.

The earth they walked on was hard and bare, stony to their moccasin-bound feet. But Ellie, being younger had coped better than her mother here. None of the 81 residents of Ahoamah were used to hard walking in this freezing weather, and their feet suffered; theirs had been an agrarian society, employed upon countryside affairs such as farming, and matters relating to religious worship. They knew no hardship like their ancestors had known.

Luckily, Najun had his medicine bag on him. He had dried herbs and ointment – cayenne, burdock and chickweed – which he applied to sore, cold feet and toes. But he didn't have much of a supply and he mentioned to his wife, Clara, that he was worried that his stock was so low. He thought that as they ventured further out he might not find the herbs he wanted. It being wintertime, only a handful of herbs could be found growing, such as burdock and horseradish.

Clara said soothingly: "I will try and collect the herbs you need; you just concentrate on making them into lotions to treat your people. Look – here comes Granny Meg. She can hardly walk!"

An old Indian woman stopped beside Clara. She had an army blanket wrapped tightly around her, but it was obvious to Clara that the woman had sore feet. "I swear to you, Clara, I can't hobble another step!"

Clara examined the woman's cold feet. She replied: "Your feet are in a bad way. You shouldn't have to walk! I'll try and get you a place on one of the wagons. But they are pretty packed already!"

A younger Indian woman was speaking to Najun. "Oooh! That cream you're putting on my foot is working a real treat! Wado!"

"I am glad something is helping!" Najun said morosely.

"But it is so cold out here!" The younger woman exclaimed. "I would give anything to be beside my large, roaring log fire at the moment!" She shivered, clutching her blanket and said, kindly, to Granny Meg, "You must be very tired now. I hope they can find you a space in one of the wagons!"

"I hope so, too. I ache all over!"

"Oh, you poor thing!"

Everyone was aware that they'd left everything behind – their possessions, their homes, and their livelihoods. None of the women had had time to pick up pots and pans or cooking utensils.

The soldiers had supplies of flour and corn, salt pork, and coffee and sugar in the trundling wagons. Chief Whiteleaf had been told that each Indian would get a just helping, but what was handed out was meager in the extreme. He remonstrated with one man who seemed to be in charge of the kitchen stock, pointing out that the soldiers didn't seem to do too badly. They had extra blankets to start with.

There had been angry outbreaks then – mostly from the younger full-blood Cherokee Indians, who had to be rounded up at gunpoint and chained. Seeing this, the elder men, although they too had muttered angrily amongst themselves, seemed to resign their anxious minds to whatever fate awaited them and gave in to the soldier's demands. They didn't camp for long that first weary day. Not many of the community had time to talk to each other or air their grievances, as they were intently watched. They were still too shocked at being run out of their town.

Being out in the icy elements took some getting used to. The keen wind was like a cold poultice on the older people's backs. They groaned when they learned that the trail they were to follow was to take them northwest to Nashville, Tennessee, then through to Hopkinville, Kentucky. They would have to cross the Mississippi River, then turn south, southwest and cross the Ozark Plateau to Oklahoma territory – a 1,000-mile march

"How are we to manage this journey?" they asked themselves. Some cried: "I can't take all this in!" Others exclaimed: "I'll never make this journey!" and "It sounds like a long, long way!"

Their despair at this intensive march upset all the Indians. Chief Whiteleaf was inundated with queries. He held up his hands. "My friends and neighbors, I can only tell you what you already know! Somehow, we must make this journey and pray that God goes with us! Be strong in your hearts! I know I can count on you all to be brave!"

It hadn't helped their morale to hear that 1500 Cherokees had died in confinement since May of that year in the army stockades deliberately built to house the refugees. Was there any hope for them?

They all complained of the cold and the fact that the army blankets did not shield them from the biting wind and snow that had begun to fall on them.

Right at the start of the journey, the soldiers had ordered the Indians to throw away their weapons, and they'd collected the hunting knives and some guns from those who reluctantly yielded.

A few younger Indians had not obeyed the order. Some still carried their weapons, craftily hidden.

One such boy was Ellie's cousin, Jobe. He showed her his knife, hidden in the lining of his buckskin waistcoat. It was only a small knife, but sharp-looking and dangerous just the same.

"Why do you keep it?" Ellie asked. "It's no good to you here."

Jobe's sister, Nancy, agreed with Ellie. She was standing next to them, a tall and very thin girl with hair in plaits. She had a narrow face, like her mother, who was sister-in-law to Alison, and she was the eldest of the group, being sixteen and older than Ellie by one year.

Jobe, grunted at their lack of interest. "I might need it; some of us have kept our weapons so that we can fight our way out if need be! When we do break out I'm going with the others!"

Nancy cried out: "Jobe, you can't – you'll get hurt!"

Jobe shrugged wide shoulders as Ellie exclaimed: "But you can't go home! The Government have stopped us returning, I know that much! Where would you go?"

"To the mountains. They wouldn't be able to spare the soldiers to trail us there."

"When would you go?" Ellie lowered her voice and her eyes as a soldier passed close beside them.

"Soon. Some of us have a plan…You'll know when it happens." Jobe's deep-set eyes shone with the energy of youth. The walking had not yet wearied him as it had some of the other members of his family.

Ellie thought about this. She liked the idea of running away. She saw herself hiding in the wild mountains, cooking on an open fire for all the escaped Indians. She stated, suddenly: "Let me come with you!"

Jobe shook his head. "This is men's work. I can't be held responsible for you as well! Be sensible, Ellie!"

"But I'll stay out of your way – I promise!"

Nancy said, sharply: "No, Ellie! You are needed here! Besides, your mama would never let you go!" Ellie realized the truth in this, but she admired Jobe's bravado, even as she wished she was going with him. Neither of them knew that Jobe would never make the mountains...

It was especially hard for the women; their babies had cried constantly during the day, their worried, unsettled mothers trying to comfort them. Alison had flitted between the groups of women at various intervals, tight-lipped and angry at the injustice of being jolted from her home, Ellie by her side, trying to help out. Martha made make-shift bundles using old shawls so that the babies could be carried by the women on their backs. It was a basic idea, but it did the trick. It left the mother free to hold hands with her younger children. The older children clung to their mother's skirts.

Martha, although tired, had shown her granddaughter what to do, whilst Alison had been elsewhere, tending to mothers who had found it difficult to walk so far carrying such a heavy bundle, wearing only the clothes that they had worn when they'd been driven out of their land.

It was no wonder at the end of this very strange, soul-destroying day, that Alison was washed-out with her efforts. Along with this physical strain was her emotional strain – she had lost her husband Willard Sheldon Starr to a gunshot wound only a year ago. A drunken fight in another saloon one night with a horse dealer had shot the life out of her man. She had driven to collect him home in the buggy knowing he would be too drunk to ride his horse, and she had witnessed the kill. That night, she'd driven home a body instead of a living person.

Only a mother could sense how low her daughter was, for Martha said to Alison in passing: "You look more tired than I am, my dear!"

Hearing the note of compassion in Martha's voice, Alison sighed. She rubbed her bold, dark eyes that Ellie had inherited, and then massaged her slender hands over her body, smoothing out her special dress she'd worn today for the meeting. With these erratic movements her blanket almost slipped off her thin shoulders. "I am. It has been a strange day! I keep thinking of that night when I took the buggy out to pick up my husband. Funny...but his death has been haunting me all day long!"

"Try not to think too much about it, daughter."

Alison began to cry softly to herself. "I can't help it! It was only last year! If only Willard had stayed home, instead of going out and picking a fight with that horse owner! I'll never forget the look on Ellie's face when I brought his body back – lying so stiff and cold! She knew something was wrong!"

As she spoke Alison could remember the fear of loss she'd felt as she bent over Willard's body, his thready voice whispering words to her as blood trickled out of his mouth. "L-look after Ellie!" he'd said, haltingly. By then, he was hardly breathing. In haste, a desperate Alison had put her mouth close to Willard's ear and murmured: "Hold on, my dear, I'll go get you a doctor. "

"Won't...make...it. Tell Ellie...love her...and...you!"

"Please, Willard! Stay with me!" There were tears in Alison's dark eyes.

But Willard's gaunt, half Indian face had relaxed, his eyes glassy.

Too late to help at the showdown, the sheriff of the town had come out as she wailed over her husband's body. He'd taken Willard's wrist and felt for a pulse. "He's gone, Ma'am."

It was the sheriff who'd helped her drag Willard onto the open buggy. He'd known Willard, being a half breed himself. A lot of the folk in this town were half-breed Cherokee and Choctaw Indians who, mostly, rubbed shoulders together quite well. But it had been a White dealer who'd shot Willard.

When she'd driven home with her husband's horse tethered to the back of the wagon, Alison could remember Ellie running out, her round eyes all lit up in anticipation of seeing her pa come home. Then Ellie saw the tied horse and the still bundle in the back of the wagon, and she knew that something bad had happened to her pa. It came to Ellie, that awful realization that she would never see her pa again and her tears had flowed, thick and fast.

Alison said now: "Ellie cried so much. I knew I'd have to honor Willard's wishes, to look after her – keep her by me. You know how tempestuous she can be – I have to keep her near me in case she does crazy things like she did when she tried to get her horse back today!"

Martha nodded. "I know what you mean! Ellie can be a wildcard sometimes! You have never spoken of how you feel before, daughter. It must be this strange day, like you said!"

"The walk has loosened my tongue, you mean! But this has been a terrible day! Oh, but I shall miss Ahoama forever!"

That night it was ferociously cold, with the threat of snow in the air, the damp chill of the evening entering everyone's bones. Even the soldiers were grumbling, rubbing their hands, their rifles and bayonets hanging uselessly in the crook of their arms.

Alison prayed for morning, calling to her God for solace, and Ellie prayed for more food. The walk had given her young body quite an appetite. She also said her prayers for her dead father. Even on this walk, she paid her devotions, believing in the Sky God, and also one whom her mother called a 'Christian God'. Some of the older members of the tribe, the girl knew, preyed to the Nunnehi, who were supposed to be a race of immortal spirit people known for their protection of the Cherokee in times of trouble.

They were lucky to go to sleep beside a fire blowing out its blue grey smoke that night. No one slept well.

When dawn came, stiff-legged and tired-eyed, their breath frosting in the cold air, they were herded west. No one knew where they were going, but by the second day they'd reached an army stockade.

Chapter Four

The Outpost

It was a small, tumbledown fort that was only meant to hold about a hundred soldiers. Instead it housed nearly three hundred Indian prisoners rounded up, as well as the soldiers left behind to guard them.

The place was cramped, and there were rats.

Ellie, her mother, and all her people were herded into the barracks enclosure that second day to be met by more morose Indian tribes, squashed into several different open-air pens, bunched together like sardines.

There was standing room only, although some Indians did manage to sleep on the floor, some not even lucky enough to have a shawl. All they had was the sky for a blanket and the hard, rutted earth for a pillow.

There was sickness here. Smallpox was rife, and pneumonia. The soldiers bullied and the children cried, hugging their mother's skirts. The dogs were kicked out, to roam the camp and scavenge for food. No one cared about them.

It was a hell hole.

Ellie and her mother were placed with their own clan – something both were grateful for.

Alison again, was tight-lipped over the injustice done to her people, but, like the men, she could do nothing, except pray to the Sky God for help.

"Why are we being kept here, Mama?" Ellie had asked, looking aghast at the suffering Indians surrounding them

Alison was already asking the nearest Indian who was from another township, a Chickasaw man who helped his wife by carrying their baby in his arms, his eyes sad and tired from lack of sleep and privacy.

She turned back to Ellie after a long conversation. "It seems this is a halfway place. We are set to travel on somewhere else – maybe in a few days. Keep away from that man, Ellie. He is sick."

Not only sick, but the Indian – another Cherokee – was old and wheezing breath sharply as he lay forlorn and helpless on the earth floor, shivering. Ellie, out of curiosity, had begun to kneel beside him to see if he was alright. Alison pulled her daughter away.

"Leave him! We can do nothing for this one! You must save your strength for yourself, daughter!"

How they got through the day, no one knew. Rations were given out. It was hard to eat the undigested fodder that passed as food, and even Ellie threw away the cornbread she was eating because it was stale and tasteless and stuck to the innards of the mouth like buffalo glue. The water given them was murky and as brackish as the food.

"If we stay here like this," Alison muttered angrily, "we'll be ill, too!"

Chief Whiteleaf had tried to remonstrate to the man who gave out the food in this outpost. It had been Nathan who'd gone and fetched him when the old chief asked for help. Alone amongst the other men, Nathan felt sorry for the Indians. So he'd quickly sought out the provisions manager.

The man grumblingly came over. He was scruffily dressed with his shirt-coat hanging over his breeches and he blinked at Chief Whiteleaf owlishly, displaying toothless gums. The Chief pulled an Indian child towards him, holding her gently by the shoulders. The little girl stared mutely up at the disinterested provisions manager, puffy eyes spilling over with unshed tears.

"See this child," Chief Whiteleaf pointed out. "She is cold and hungry. Soon, she will have little strength! She must have hot food and milk!"

The little girl wailed: "A – ya uyosi!" (I hungry!)

The man tried to chew his lip. Without his teeth, that wasn't an easy thing to do. "Can't help that, Injun. Ah don't give my stock to all you Injuns jus' because a kid needs feedin'. Ah gotta feed you all at the right time. She'll git what you all git an' that's that!"

"Then I'll speak with your captain."

Nathan cut in with: "He ain't here. He's gone on a-head t'map out the journey."

"There must be someone I can talk to! We are all starving here!"

Nathan had the grace to look worried. "Ah'm sorry; Ah'd help you if Ah could—"

The provisions manager butted in: "Go away, old-timer." He pushed Chief Whiteleaf brusquely with the tip of his long-barreled colt. "Don't a-bother us again!"

As if sensing that she'd been refused food the little girl began to cry harder. Ellie, who'd been standing amongst the crowd around Chief Whiteleaf, came forward and led the child away leaving the chief with his hands on his hips, his lips pursed. It seemed that even here he could do nothing to help his people.

Nathan noticed the Indian girl with a sudden flash of interest. He thought how striking she looked.

Unlike the others, Ellie's face was flushed and lively, and he was aware of her earthly charm and femininity.

Apart from rounding them up on their home ground, it was the first time Nathan had been amongst the Indians again and he held them in awe – their fine, but dirty western-style clothes, their air of solidarity. To him, they were exotic creatures from another world. Again, he felt sorry for them and how they were being treated by the rough-necked soldiers. But, as one man he could do nothing about it.

They were guarded savagely. The Indians were just clubbed or butted with the soldier's rifles, or threatened with the mean end of a bayonet, if they tried to remonstrate. Blood in the wind, their new resting place was a bitter abode to be in, here sickness and dysentery was rife.

Two days passed, and then lengthened to a week. By this time Alison's best dress was filthy, covered with the mud from the dirt floor, and the fringe on Ellie's red hemp underskirt had become course and twisted. The fug of life and unwashed bodies flooded over everyone in the vicinity of the pens. Even the cold could not hide the smell.

They saw the tall blond captain, McGinty, only once, when he made his rounds on the second day of their stay. He spoke little; surveyed the people through half-closed, disinterested eyes, and then he'd turned away. But one thing he did do was tell his men to remove the bodies of the dead – those who'd died in the night, including the wheezy old Indian whom Ellie had first seen lying still on the floor.

They also removed a dead man whom Ellie knew vaguely as Solomon. One of the soldiers had shot him. Blood had spattered Ellie's knee as she'd been close nearby, when, in the night Solomon had picked a fight with another tribal member, trying to drag a blanket off of a Choctaw Indian.

"Iss mine! You stole it!" He'd shouted.

The other Indian had retaliated with a sideways swipe at Solomon whilst trying to retain his meager piece of shawl that had once belonged to a woman and which he was using as a blanket.

"That shawl was my wife's!" Solomon hissed, lunging again, clutching at the material and dragging it. Those grouped nearby, including Ellie and Alison had no room to move away from the fighting men.

One of the guards rushed over at the disturbance. "Stop that, or I fire, Injun!"

Maddened, the Indian took no notice. The guard raised his rifle, as did several others at the same time. Their blasts reverberated through the packed crowd and some of the Indian women cowered back against the rails of the pen, unable to breath, gunsmoke in their nostrils. Solomon slumped, slashed to ribbons by gunfire, his hand still clutching the material he'd been so desperate to retrieve.

The soldiers had hauled his dead body outside the pen and had left it in the dirt, which soon turned a rusty red.

Many from Ahoama took their troubles to Chief Whiteleaf, but he could do nothing to help them. "The Government has promised us a new land where we will be given axes to chop up wood and build our homes. According to the federal state, we have been given blankets and food – but that is an understatement, for we now know how bad conditions are for us here. I have tried to remonstrate, but the captain and his soldiers do not listen to what I ask for! Even I say that it is useless to talk to them!"

Someone suggested: "Let the priest talk to them!"

Chief Whiteleaf had shaken his long, grey-haired head. "Frank is busy helping to bury those who died yesterday," he said.

An Indian from the crowd called out: "That's not fair! He seems to be the only man allowed out of here!"

Chief Whiteleaf shrugged. "That is his job!"

Some one else shouted: "We must do something! The conditions are so bad here!"

"I am sorry," Chief Whiteleaf replied. "But there is nothing I can do, unless anyone here has any suggestions?"

No one else had any further proposals. Everyone present felt frustrated that they couldn't get away from this ill-fortified stockade.

The next day, soldiers awoke them. One of the soldiers exclaimed: "Phew! What a stink!"

His friend replied: "What d'ye expect? They've been cooped up here for the last week and more!"

The first soldier merely shouted at the dazed Indians. "Alright, everybody up! We're movin' out! Get into queues! You – fellow – move! Or I'll stick you with this bayonet!"

Chief Whiteleaf grunted. "I am moving! I am moving! What is happening? Where are we going?"

"Jus' get into line, old-timer! We're a-going t'be counting all of you!"

"You're splitting us up?

"Sure thing!"

Chief Whiteleaf looked around for his family and shouted: "Martha! Alison! Where's Ellie? ...Oh, there you are! Ellie, get Rachel, Nancy and Jobe! We're moving out! Everyone must stay together!"

Taken by surprise, the tired Indians were rounded up in the chill morning and the whole camp was sorted into, roughly, a hundred men, woman and children at a time. Each shuffling group was given a leader to guide them and fresh rations to feed them. Split into thirteen sections everyone had a different route to follow.

Ellie, Alison and their family were allocated to Captain McGinty's section. They had no choice but to follow his orders, although those in other groups were actually led by their own Indian people, and some were led by hired contractors who were paid $65 for food and medicines for each person in their care. Money, the Indians knew, that would never be used for its intended purpose.

Sullenly, with several refugees already tired and ill, for many had chills and fevers from exposure and the change of country, with cursing wagon masters and groaning wheels, the Indians began their real walk. The exodus had begun...

Chapter Five

The Journey

That was how it was all the time from then on; more and more walking. None of the Indians in Ellie and Alison's clan knew the names of this wilderness area they had started to travel through. They passed townships that were unfamiliar to them, and were watched by the settlers. Some days they were marched into a new fort and penned up again, which left the Indians in very low spirits.

The savage cold ripped through them all and they were very hungry. They often glanced up in apprehension at the lowering sky, which was gunmetal grey, whilst the mountains surrounding them stood out, etched in a sharp white relief.

From time to time, Ellie thought she saw a grey wolf following them. He kept well into the background, and she could see that he looked like an old wolf with patchy fur. He just seemed curious about the straggling groups of people shambling along in his territory, and she dismissed him from her mind, concentrating on the walk.

As the long wave of straggling Indians wound their way on they were guarded by the soldiers, some on foot and some on horseback, their little ponies wiry and tough, protected by their hairy coat against the harsh chill, their breath billowing clouds of moisture in the crystal cold air.

The food situation was bad; supplies were scarce and, before they could reach a river , they often went days without water. Sometimes, they had to get by on just one meal a day.

There were no roads to travel over and some of the hardier men and women went ahead to cut timber out of the way with axes when their route became impassable.

The ox wagons slowly rumbled along carrying food, blankets,

bedding and those elderly folk that were not able to walk too far, or who were crippled, or sick.

The little children cried day after day from weariness, hunger and illness. Death soon began to stalk everyone and not just the weak.

The walk was beyond human endurance, yet they plodded on, dying by the hundreds, being buried by the roadside every day. When streams were crossed, the water often came up to the chins of the men and women who had to walk. They would hold their children head high and wade forward grimly. It was a seemingly endless march for a weary, struggling mass of humanity.

Each family did its own cooking on the road from the supplies they received from the food wagons. They didn't have matches so they started their fires by rubbing two flint rocks together and catching the spark on a piece of dry spunk held directly underneath the rocks. Often, they would have to rake away the snow to clear a place to build their fires. When they could get dry wood they carried it in the overburdened government wagons which creaked and groaned their way up the various hills that they had to pass through. Those who walked through the snow became footsore and weary in their soon tattered and torn Sunday-best clothes. Some had to make the trip barefoot and often left bloody footprints in the snow.

The Indians were joined by other tribes who had also been rounded up. Of the 14,000 men, woman and children many had come from such tribes as the Chickasaw, the Seminole and the Choctaw groups, all wading unhappily along the track. Again, at this point, they were separated into fresh groups. Alison and Ellie were still together. But Rachel and Nancy were almost separated.

One of the indifferent soldiers had seized Nancy, who had been standing quietly by herself, and thrust her in with a group of Choctaw Indians.

Dragged by the waist, she screamed out: "Ma! He's taking me away! Help me!" Rachel, hearing her cry, ran forward and immediately flung herself on the soldier. Like Alison, she was desperate to keep her family together. Also, like Alison, Rachel had lost her man. But he had died of Smallpox. That had been several years ago. She had never taken another husband, although the chance was there. Jobe had become the man of the family then, a title that he lived up to, even at the age of eleven.

"Let her go! She's my daughter! She stays with me!"

Fending her off with one hand the soldier was panting with his exertions. "Don' matter who yer with, do it? All you Indians look alike t'me! Quit kicking you black-tailed bitch!" Nancy was swinging her legs as hard as she could, whilst trying to twist away from his grip. With Rachel dragging on her daughter's hand he was hard put to it to hold the wriggling girl, the struggling, determined mother and his rifle at the same time!

The commotion encouraged McGinty to stride over. He surveyed the struggle with a slight grin on his face.

Rachel appealed to him. "He has no right to separate my daughter from me!"

"How old is she?"

"She's only twelve!" Rachel lied.

McGinty scrutinized her a moment. "Wouldn't be lying would 'cha?"

Rachel met his eyes.

"She's mighty tall for a twelver!" McGinty decided.

Rachel blinked, but said nothing. Nancy had stopped struggling, but the soldier still grasped her tightly.

McGinty turned to the girl. "Your age. What is it, gal?"

Nancy also held his eagle-eyed stare bravely. "Please! I'm twelve!"

"Hhmmph!"

Rachel spoke sharply. "She's too young to leave me! She ain't a boy!"

McGinty slid his hands into his overcoat pockets, elbows tucked out comfortably. He was just going to make a decision

33

when, like a whirlwind, Jobe erupted beside his mother, his eyes hot and intense. "What's happening?" His hands were clenched as he took in the scene, the soldier gripping his sister and the still, watchful expression on Rachel's face.

Jobe swung on McGinty: "Let my sister go, or I'll hit you!"

McGinty threw back his head and guffawed, his eyes full of a sardonic amusement.

"Hah! You're mighty sure of yourself! You're not even tall enough t'swing a blow at me!"

There was general mocking laughter from a group of McGinty's men who'd stopped their work to watch Jobe's humiliation.

Jobe saw red. He bowed his head and prepared to stampede this tall, rangy man who dared to make him look foolish. He ran forward and swung a fast fist at McGinty. McGinty adroitly caught the fist in a steely grip and brought the boy's arm back behind his shoulder, pushing it up hard so that Jobe grimaced in pain.

McGinty said: "Get the message, injun... Ah'm stronger than you! Unless you want to fight me?

Jobe muttered something. McGinty, grinning broadly, shook him. "What's that you say?""I said: 'There's nothing better I'd rather do!'"

McGinty shook Jobe again, enjoying himself. His men laughed.

"How shall we do it, boy? Fisticuffs?"

"You bet, you big tall bug!"

MgGinty's men laughed again. McGinty grinned.

Rachel intervened: "Leave my boy alone!"

McGinty glanced at her, becoming serious again. "Only if he tells me the truth! Now – how old is your sister?"

Still held with his hand behind his back, Jobe's eyes swerved to his mother. Her anxious glance carried a message to him. Jobe sensed it. He glanced at Nancy, and as McGinty released him he scratched his head. "Dunno... Why should I tell you anyway? Take away your title and you're only a common soldier – like the rest of 'em!"

McGinty's eyes flashed. He cuffed Jobe with his gloved hand. "Cork your mouth, boy! Cheekin' me doesn't pay!"

Rachel moved forward a step, her eyes boiling.

Jobe pretended to look cowed. He cried: "It's no good asking me how old my sister is! I can't count, you hear!"

Rachel also put her hands on her hips and came to her son's rescue. "It' true! He's had no schooling. He hasn't learned numbers n' things! Leave my poor boy be! I want my daughter to stay with me! She shouldn't be separated from her family!"

McGinty sighed. He was rapidly getting bored with this situation, and he had other work to do than waste any more time on these Indians. To the soldier who held onto Nancy, he ordered: "Let the gal go. If it pleases 'em it pleases me. Ah don't want anymore uncommon squabbles – we've enough Injuns to see to!"

Nancy wrenched herself free from the soldier's slack hand and immediately went and stood beside her mother. With his usual nonchalance, McGinty turned away and left them.

Rachel hugged her daughter, sending a few daggers of distrust after the soldier who'd tried to tear Nancy away from her.

"Well done, Jobe! He isn't to know how good your counting really is!" she told her son in a quick whisper, as other soldiers rounded them up and sorted out their group. "I'm proud of my learned boy!"

Nancy was glad to see she was in the same section as Alison and Ellie, who put her arms around her cousin; thankful herself that no one was to be separated. At least, now, they could stay together. As the two girls hugged each other, Ellie again noticed the patchy grey wolf hovering in the shadowy background. A couple of soldiers threw snowy stones at it, but the creature just wandered away and popped up somewhere else, watching them with incurious eyes.

Their next march forward began and some of the older Indian women were allowed to travel in the wagons, holding babies and very small infants, helping those mothers who couldn't carry their children anymore. They wore blankets wrapped around their pinched, wan faces, their seamed eyes as dull as the weather. Their partners sat beside them, holding the reins, their large, floppy hats pulled well down over their foreheads, shielding their faces from the withering wind.

The line of men and women trudged along the men walking with bowed heads whilst the woman had their hands full, keeping the older, errant children close to them.

There were some camp dogs that had survived the fort internment ambling beside them, with ears down and tails tucked under. They looked as dejected and downcast as their masters were. If the wolf had been around then the dogs might have tried to chase after it, but they were too weak, and as hungry, dispirited and tired as the Indians were.

In one instance, at a very rough, frosted, churned up section of road, the front wheel broke away from one of the cooking wagons and it lurched sideways, stuck in a deep rut. The oxen pulling the cart collapsed under the weight of the wheel falling on its hind leg. The wagon tipped drunkenly sideways. The beast brayed in pain, its leg broken.

Ellie put her hands to her ears, not liking to hear the animal in such physical discomfort. Soldiers and Indians were swarming around the wagon. The driver and his wife were being helped up off the dirt by their friends, looking bedraggled and dazed.

A cage-load of live grouse had fallen out the back of the wagon along with some beaver pelts that the Indians were hoping to barter with at the next township, and the plump birds were running around squeaking and squawking with some of the younger Indian children chasing after them.

McGinty rode up, took stock of the situation. "Shoot the beast!" He pointed to the oxen but no one heard him in the commotion. He swung down from his horse, grabbed his own rifle and marched swiftly towards the pain-crazed animal, ready to put it out of its misery.

In all this confusion young Indians stole some of the food supplies that had slid out of the wagon's flap opening, trying to slip away before any of the soldiers noticed.

But some were seen.

"Hey!" A soldier shouted. "Them Injuns are stealing the supplies!"

McGinty swung round, rifle in hand. He sighted a running Indian, took stock and aimed to fire. His shot missed. The Indian swerved, fell over in his haste to get away with the food. McGinty fired again. The Indian fell, dead.

Immediately, a battle raged. There were outbreaks of anger as soldiers and Indians clawed at the provisions and attacked each other, trying to avenge their brother's death.

Ellie saw a guard knock a man down who had been trying to make a getaway, some wrapped up rabbit meat held under his arm. This brought several Indians surging towards the soldier, shouting at him.

"Leave him alone; he is my brother!" A tall, thickset Indian hurled a knotted fist at the soldier. It missed as the man stepped tensely back, keeping his rifle up and well-aimed.

The Indian looked like he was going to throw another punch, rifle or no, but the soldier moved in first, using his weapon to swipe at the Indian's outraged face.

He drew blood and the man staggered sideways under the hit. This brought more Indians surging around the soldier and for a moment, he was in danger of being cut off from the other guards.

But others had seen the incident and had now joined in the melee. It was a mix of soldiers and Indians shouting and struggling with each other until several soldiers, standing firm together, fired a volley of gun shots into the air.

Ellie had been standing nearest to the deafening noise and she froze. In her hands she held some food, intending to pass it to the Indian standing next to her. She could see that more soldiers had come and the Indians were hemmed in a tight circle with bayonets pointing at them.

McGinty was marching towards her, a purposeful look on his long face. "It's you again! Put it down, drat you! It doesn't belong to you!"

Ellie was afraid of him, but she put on a bold front and stood her ground stubbornly.

"Its food you've purloined from us, Tall Man! We have a right to it!"

For answer, McGinty snatched the food out of her hands, his green eyes glittering, and his blond moustache bristling. He planted his long body squarely in front of her. Of his own accord he took hold of her face with one hand. Ellie tried to flinch away but his fingers remained hooked around her jaw. He bent down slightly and looked into her defiant eyes.

"You could be whipped for this! What d'ye mean by it, taking our grub!" He let go of her face and Ellie found her voice and cried: "We're all hungry! You don't give us enough food!"

"All of you will have to learn to eat less, missy!"

Chief Whiteleaf, seeing his grandchild in trouble, had pushed his way through the circle of bayonets.

"My granddaughter is right; many times I have asked you for more food – there just isn't enough to go round. Walking makes us hungrier."

"There'll be more grub at the next stop. The Government has lain in provisions for us with the farmers. Until then – you all go hungry—" McGinty broke off suddenly, seeing, out of the corner of his vision, an Indian running for the hills.

"Ah can't allow this!" he muttered, and he threw the food to another soldier and ran for his horse. He swung onto it and kicked the animal into action. His rifle in his hand, he lost no time in catching up with the errant Indian, a Choctaw boy who, like Jobe, had a concealed Bowie knife on his person.

McGinty called: "Halt – or I fire!"

The Indian dived for a snow-covered boulder. McGinty's bullet hit the rocks with a pinging sound. "Come out, Injun', with your hands up!"

He aimed his rifle again, found the trigger had jammed, cursed the weapon and swung down from his horse, walking steadily toward the rock with a Colt in his hand.

The Indian pounced from the top of the rock, landing on McGinty's shoulder, arm raised.

His knife came down. McGinty caught the Indian's brown, supple wrist, held the knife away, grunting with the effort. The two rolled over onto the patchy snow together, and the gun dropped from McGinty's grasp as he struggled for his life.

The Indian boy was fierce and strong, used to dealing with his quarry with stealth and cunning. He used all the tactics he could, but McGinty, trained soldier that he was, knew all the maneuvers. He parried, blocked, and knocked the knife from the youngster's steely grip against the sharp rock. It clattered away to be hidden by a small snowdrift. Now straddling the Indian boy, McGinty used an iron fist and threw a hefty punch at the boy that would have knocked a mule over. It made contact and he swiftly avenged another blow that knocked the Indian out cold. Staggering up, breathing hard, McGinty whistled for reinforcements.

By this time more soldiers had come running to join the scene and the Indians, though roused and still angry and bitter, were being herded roughly back into line, order once more being resumed.

Under McGinty's commands the Oxen was hauled away and its remains butchered by the chopping man – one of McGinty's 'kitchen' soldiers.

Whilst all this was going on McGinty sent out scouts to find a wheelwright. When they did manage to find one they camped for a long time until the wheel could be put back on and made strong enough to haul the wagon.

Chapter Six

Shadow of the Eagle/Medicine Man

Evening was upon them by then. They stayed camped in the same place, out in the open. Everyone sat listlessly with their backs to the wagons beside their fires, arms folded against the chill. The women went about scrounging what food they could get from the soldiers who were handing out jerky and water from the wagons, leaving tired, dirty children to fall asleep, limbs twitching in their dreams.

Wood smoke drifted towards the dark sky, those near the fires hazily watched the crackling flames whilst others stretched out, preparing for sleep.

Helping the people to bed down for the night was Frank, the half-blood preacher man. He had been brought up amongst the Cherokees in Ahoamah since he was a baby. His American mother had worked in Ahoamah as a Missionary, and she'd met and married Thomas Saunders, a full-blood Cherokee there. Frank's mother was very religious and she'd passed this gene onto her offspring. Frank grew up in the church and wanted nothing more but to be a man of the cloth.

When he did become a preacher, he taught the townspeople Christian beliefs. He was a quiet man who spoke little, but he helped a lot. He was doing this now, holding lanterns into wagons so that the women could see to tuck up their tired children against the cold, making them as snug as they could against the chill wind of the night. When he'd done this, Frank wandered around and found a place for himself to bed down where he knew that others could find him if they needed him. Despite the hard ground he was soon asleep.

The evening was still, cold and silent, the wind whispering its throaty chorus through the scrubland. Everyone – the soldiers included – was tired and stiff. No one took notice of a young white-tail buck as it skirted their camp, stopping now and then to lift a dainty nose, sniffing the night air.

But it had left its scent to be followed, and followed it was – slowly, nimbly, padding lithely, a predator was loose...

Following only its prey a cougar stalked by, its eyes gleaming in the dark with yellow intent.

The frightened deer snorted, knowing it was being tailed, and suddenly darted into the camp, startling Jobe, who was leaning near a boulder watching his family bed down for the night. Nancy was helping her mother tuck some of the babies up in the wagons.

The deer also startled several of the soldiers' horses and some of the mules that had been tied up nearby. One horse neighed loudly, rolling its eyes and trying to back away from its halter rope attached to a tree branch. The movement snapped the halter and the horse bolted.

Jobe saw the horse break loose and he was up and running after it before he had time to think what he was doing and he came face to face with the cougar.

Thinking it was a bob-cat, he yelled: "Ga hey! Ga hey!" He let go of the horse's dangling bridle, hearing his sister's sudden, high-pitched scream. He smelt the feral scent of the animal and saw its gaping fangs. In a frightened frenzy the horse streaked off and the buck the cougar had been stalking sprinted away as well.

There was a shout behind him as others noticed the crouching cat, but Jobe's wide eyes were on the cougar, as denied its original prey, it snarled at him and made ready to pounce.

In all his short young life Jobe was not prepared for this moment. He only knew that the cat meant to attack him and he couldn't believe that it was happening, for cougars were usually shy and elusive around men. The knife he'd hidden from the soldiers came into his hand as he remembered it and rummaged for it, tearing it forcefully, urgently from the lining of his jacket, and he raised it in a hopeless, fearful gesture of defense as the heavy creature sprung at him, knocking him to the ground in a powerful surge.

The knife came down, stabbing warm fur, the cat slashed and hissed and Jobe screamed with the red-hot pain. He felt the animal's breath on his face and he raised his arms, shrinking from this dangerous, devilish onslaught, feeling the creature on top of him, biting, tearing flesh, as he tried to beat it off.

The soldiers and some younger Indians came running with sticks of fire, warding off the snarling, ferocious cat as Jobe writhed in agony.

The cougar's baleful eyes glared at them in defiance, but it backed away, hissing, then it suddenly sprang to the right and flung its eight-foot-long length into the river nearby, swimming easily and powerfully across. It was injured, but not as badly as Jobe was. It left the Indians on the bank, their flaming torches lighting up the scrubland around them with an eerie glow.

Ellie and Alison, alerted by all the shouting and the commotion came and stood by watching Jobe writhe about, helplessly clutching his arm and chest, whilst Nancy tried to keep the bloodstained boy as still as possible.

Ellie's mother turned to her with sharp eyes. "Get Najun – quickly!"

Ellie sprinted off, her keen sight enabling her to see well in the semi-darkness made by the glow of the torch-lights.

She ran into McGinty before she could stop herself.

"Wow-ah – who's this?" He caught hold of her elbows and peered downwards. "Oh, it's you – Ellie – isn't it? Why are you running round like an arrow's been shot in your rump?!"

Ellie gasped: "We need the medicine man! Jobe's been attacked by a cougar!"

"A cougar! They don't often go for humans! What's the boy been do'in that a danged cougar attacks him?"

"I don't know!" she wailed. "But I must get help for him! Let me go!"

He released her and she sprinted past him like a whirlwind. McGinty calmly walked over to where the crowd of Indians stood.

Ellie soon spotted their medicine man. He was wrapped in a brown shawl, thin head covered, snoring peacefully, partially propped up against a wagon wheel. His wife Clara was asleep in one of the wagons.

Ellie shook him awake roughly and without any respect for his age. His lined face snapped up to meet her urgent stare as she shouted at him: "You're wanted! Over there! Jobe's been attacked!"

Slowly, the old man rose to his feet, his shawl dropping to his shoulders, revealing a long lock of dark grey hair tumbling down his high, bony forehead, fastened with a single eagle's feather and some rough-made beads.

He had deep, cavernous sunk black eyes that took in all details and as he moved his thin neck to where Ellie pointed, his round, global earrings shone like copper in his ears.

"Najun!" Someone else called his name in passing, and he roused himself to follow Ellie.

Jobe had a group of women around him, including his thoroughly alarmed sister and mother, and also Martha. Najun passed them, his eyes upon the boy, assessing his wounds, which were bleeding ferociously.

"Get water!" A women nearest to him scurried away to quickly do his bidding.

They had no bandages. Under Najun's advice, several of the women tore off items of their clothing and with this they bound Jobe's wounds after washing them as gently as they could with the ice-cold water as the boy moaned and wriggled under their touch. Najun used an herbal ointment mix of cramp bark, chamomile, and elder.

By this time Chief Whiteleaf had joined the group. Frank was also there; it was he who had run to Clara to ask for Najun's bag of herbs. They all stood patiently, watching silently as Najun made sure that Jobe's wounds were fastened properly. He had covered Jobe with his own shawl, and as McGinty watched skeptically, ready to intervene should it be necessary, Najun, took a pouch from around his neck, and placed several items that looked like stones upon Jobe's trembling body. The stones were roughly egg-shaped and smooth to the touch. Najun took from his forehead the single eagle feather and held it aloft above Jobe's pain-filled face.

He brushed the feather away from the boy's frightened gaze, moving it around his body in a clockwise direction, sometimes stopping by the bandaged wounds and giving an extra jerk to the feather, as if trying to probe, or flick away the damaged and torn flesh.

Then he produced a rattle made of gourd and clay that had been attached to his belt, which he began to shake over the boy's body.

The silvery sound filled the night air, seemed to hang above the knot of Indians surrounding the scene. As they watched the sound intensified, blending in with everyone's heartbeat, and the old medicine man shut his eyes and began to hum softly, in tune with the rattle shaking, his thin, wiry hands moving back and forth, hovering over Jobe like a cloud.

Jobe's eyes slid shut whilst Nancy held his hand tightly, anxiously. The rattle sounded far away as he met the darkness, his pinched grey face relaxing into shocked sleep, the pain receding as if a magic wand had been waved over him.

As if pulled by some unseen string, Najun rose to his feet, eyes closed, still humming. He began to dance in a small circle next to Jobe, still shaking the rattle. Where his energy came from no one knew as his booted feet began to move faster and faster, and the rattling sound got louder and louder as the medicine man began to pitch and sway crazily from side to side, as if in a trance. Lost in music of his own making he twirled and skirled like a spinning top, not stumbling once or even skipping a beat with his rattle. A whirling banshee to all appearances he seemed to become one with the thunderous dance so that those watching could not tell whether he was a human being or not.

High above the watcher's heads a patch of the velvety night sky became lighter, greyer, even a streaky blue color. It created a kind of marbled effect. No one saw this strange phenomenon rolling across, nor did they see something suddenly appear from it and swoop down, landing on a swaying branch...

Only Ellie, out of the corner of her eye caught the swift movement. Astonished, she noticed that a large Golden Eagle was spreading its magnificent seven-foot wings out, talons balanced evenly on a bare branch above her, its imperious beak and piercing eyes glaring at them. She couldn't be sure but she thought she saw around the eagle a golden glow as if this bird was a supernatural being. Ellie was surprised that it wasn't migrating, but some eagles, she knew, stayed in their nesting territory all year.

She had to turn her head sharply, straining to see in the darkness around her, for that wasn't all she thought she saw and she wondered if she was experiencing a vision, which she did sometimes, especially when she had been younger.

It looked as if the forest behind her was moving! No. It was shapes that she saw – or thought she saw – dark shapes coming out of the wood, silhouettes of men, creeping shadows, seeming to slink out of the trees as if some ancient ritual had summoned them. The light emanating from around the eagle now seemed to embrace the shadowy figures and as she looked on, in startled amazement, she realized that they were Indian warriors of old, carrying weapons. As she stared harder it seemed that the whole forest behind the ghostly warriors lit up like a rainbow, swirls of color mingling together in a wonderful kaleidoscope of shifting shapes and images. She blinked hard because she couldn't see the familiar landscape anymore – it had vanished! But the ancient ones still stood before her, seemingly poised on the threshold of eternity. To her consternation and sudden horror, it looked as if they were starting to walk towards her.

A scream caught in her throat. She went to tug at her mother's arm, and in the same moment, Najun stopped his dance and dropped his rattle on the ground. Ellie glanced down at the sleeping Jobe and his silent head-bowed sister beside him and noticed that the stones that had been placed on his bandaged chest had gone. There was no time to wonder where. The medicine man slumped and fell and as others rushed to help him up, Ellie felt a cool breeze brush past her cheek. Something touched her that was deeper than time, older than antiquity. It was as if the ancient one's she'd thought she'd seen were around her, passing through her very being, intently watching the young Indian boy lying in a blood-soaked sleep upon the ground.

Then she was aware that something else had flown past her. She glanced up. The eerie big bird, the eagle, was now soaring skywards towards, what she now saw, was a patch of blue. The eagle carried something in its huge talons that could crush and kill a prey, and it flew straight through the blue boundary. As it did so, she actually saw the skies close together, as if someone had buttoned up a coat. No one else seemed to have noticed this unusual happening except her.

She shivered, and it wasn't the cold that caused it. The night sky had returned, dark, dreary, a storm-sodden blackness, and as she looked down at Jobe's still body, she knew in her heart that Jobe was dead, and tears pricked her eyes.

Chapter Seven

Nathan

As they moved on, one by one, friends, family and relatives succumbed to the agony of the journey, either becoming too exhausted to move a step further, fainting from hunger, or falling sick, or dying from some debilitating disease. Those who were too ill or sick to move were given a jug of water and left to die.

Every day, from then on, crosses were erected along the rough track; sometimes, not even crosses – just funeral mounds, hastily and tiredly dug. Some of the dead were placed between two logs and covered roughly with shrubs. Some were quickly shoved under thickets and many were left dead but unburied.

Martha took pity on a baby who'd died on the journey. She said, to the crying mother: "Come – let me take your baby!"

"NO!" The suffering woman moved away from Martha's outstretched arms. "No one touches my baby! She is cold – that's all! We are all cold! She'll wake up in a minute, wanting a feed!"

Martha spoke gently. "She has gone to Heaven's arms, my dear... Give her to me. I'll bury her for you. Then you can grieve properly."

"I tell you, she is alright!"

"Then why are you crying so much?"

"Because I, because...she's, she's – oh!"

Martha nodded. "Let me take her from you. I'll hold her very gently."

The woman looked down with love at the dead baby's face, which was all that could be seen from a jumble of fur and blankets. She murmured: "You're a little chick-a-buddy, aren't you? I wish you were playing a game with me! Oh, if only you could wake up!" Tears began to form in her eyes. Martha could see the grief in them.

She said quickly: "Your baby's at peace now."

The woman asked, suddenly: "Where's the preacher man? I want him here!"

"He is burying others."

With a great sob the woman suddenly placed her baby in Martha's arms. "Take her! Do what you must!"

Martha nodded. "You are very brave. You've done the right thing. Now, let us do this together... The ground is hard, but I have the broken shaft of an old hunting knife. We can bury your baby and put her to sleep. Over there would be a good place."

"You think so?"

"I know so. God will bless her there!"

The mother asked bitterly: "What god?" and she began to cry in earnest this time.

Frank came upon them. He looked very, very tired. There were deep lines running down his open-humored face, but he still placed a compassionate hand on the sobbing woman's shoulder. "I'm here now, Martha. Let me take the little mite whilst you work." His voice remained gentle – like a hushed wind. To the bereaved woman, he said: "God is always with us."

But the woman shook her head, saying: "I can't stay to watch this!" She waddled away, her family coming towards her to give her comfort.

Ellie approached them. She saw the anguished woman and made to go off after her, but Martha stopped her. "Leave her, Ellie. I know you mean well, but she needs to be alone with her family."

Ellie nodded. She was bursting with suppressed news. "I've heard that some awful bad things have been happening in another camp!"

Frank chimed in uneasily: "It is only rumor, Ellie..."

Ellie ignored him. "They say that there was a baby that wouldn't stop crying and one of the soldiers picked it up by its feet and smashed its head against a tree trunk! How dreadful is that?"

Martha gasped. "That is really terrible! Terrible! How true is this, Frank?"

"It is a rumor, nothing more!"

Martha looked sternly at Ellie. "Then forget about it! Help me cover this poor baby!"

Frank said a prayer for the piteous bundle that they laid to rest.

Ellie was glad that they weren't in any of the other groups; being in McGinty's was bad enough. He ruled his commands over everyone, then turned away as if he'd run out of steam.

Najun and Clara became disconsolate because they couldn't find the right herbs to help their people with. Najun's medicine bag was running low and he only had small bottles of 'foot' ointment and dried herbs left.

Some of the Muskogee Indians who walked with them were broken hearted too. Their woman sang songs to raise their spirits: "We are going to our homes and land; there is one who is above and forever watches over us; he will care for us."

Some prayed: "Deliver us from the jaws of death." And others cried: "Lo-ord, have mercy on us! Please remove this sorrow! What have we done to deserve this terrible ordeal!"

But it didn't help and they fell silent, for some loved one gone – some vast, treasured memory expelled forever into the mist and darkness and despair that now seemed to engulf those that were left to walk on – with no aim, no thought, no future prospects. It was a silent shuffle.

It seemed that the earth cried with them. The Indians cried, and Alison and Ellie cried, their hands and feet aching with the searing relentless cold, their tummies churning with hunger, their empty stomachs rubbing against their backbones. They couldn't even clasp their blankets around them properly as their fingers were too numb to hold the rough material together.

A never-ending story, yet each day turned for them as they

were driven on by the silent soldiers, their moccasins in tatters, their feet scratched and sore from the rough terrain. Sometimes, Ellie caught a glimpse of the old grey wolf following them. She called him 'Ghost' because he looked like a spirit wolf. In her mind she wondered if this creature was real or not, or whether she was hallucinating. But, judging by the soldiers ribald remarks the animal was flesh and blood to them. Some of the soldiers had even tried to leave meat for it.

"Look-ee... That wolf is back again!" one of the soldiers had cried out to the others, and several of them had come to see this lone predator who dared to follow their camp.

"He's after more food!"

"Throw him your meat, Turk!"

"He looks mighty hungry!"

The Wolf stood on higher ground, watching them. One soldier threw a bone that had some meat left on it; the wolf scampered away. But, as they watched, he came back for it after a while.

"Reckon if we leave him scraps o' food, he'll visit us regular."

"Yeah! We'll do that! He can become our lucky mascot!"

"Jeez! We can sure use some luck out here! This is the longest an' coldest damn march Ah've ever been on!"

Nathan had spoken briefly to Ellie, seeing that she was friendlier and more forthcoming to those around her than the rest of the clan were.

She had been dipping the dirty parts of her mother's shawl in the cold water of a creek that was situated not far from a Fort. The Indians had stopped at an old Barn where food and other provisions were supposed to await them. But some supply stations were not always filled up. The suppliers were only ordinary farmers hired by the Government to provide corn and oats and many cheated on the Indians, leaving them with only half the provisions that they should have.

Nancy was with Ellie, washing her hands along with her Mother Rachel. Since Jobe's death the two rarely spoke several words to Ellie – or the other Indians. They were very subdued and still mourned the bright-eyed youngster.

The water gurgled by with icy spikes in it, and the fir trees opposite swayed in the cool wind. Ellie had been checking the shawl for further stains, when Nathan had come upon them and spoken kindly to her:

"Ah wouldn't wet it anymore. It will never dry if you do."

Surprised by the attention, Ellie had almost dropped the shawl into the water.

"Maybe not," she spoke shyly. "But at least my mama will have a cleaner shawl to wear in a few days' time! The blanket she has does not keep out the cold!"

"Yep. It's too cold here, ain't it?"

"I keep hoping it will get warmer. We are not used to this! So many people are dying from chills and sickness. All my people! I cannot bear it!"

"Neither can Ah. Ah think it t'aint fair, what's happening to your people." At least, she realized, this young man was being thoughtful and kind.

She asked, without shyness this time, "What is your name? I have not noticed you before?"

"Ah'm called Nathan."

"I am Ellie."

"A'm mighty pleased to meet you, Ellie. You're the chief's granddaughter, aren't you?"

"I am."

He heard the pride in her voice. "Ye-es, Ah thought so. He's a noble man."

Ellie looked surprised. "You've noticed! That is kind of you to say so; many of the soldier's don't talk to us, except to give orders and push us on!"

"Guess Ah'm not like that. Ah'm not an Indian hater! But some of us aren't too bad! Ah've seen quite a few soldiers cry over your folk's sad losses. You might know Bill Hicks?"

"I think so. Is he the very thickset man with the greyish beard?"

"Yep – he gave his overcoat to a sick Indian child the other night, an' he walked around on guard duty wearing only his shirtsleeves!"

"I heard about that. He must have been really cold! He's a game man!"

"Yep, he's a good man – a good friend of mine. Some of us care, Ellie."

"Nathan!" someone called.

Nathan had been so intent on talking to this beautiful girl, that he looked behind him almost guiltily. He noticed another young soldier walking towards him, slightly bow-legged.

"Yeah?"

"Where's that firewood you're supposed to be a-fetchin'?"

"Ah, yeah... I'll go get it now."

The other soldier gave Ellie a sly look. He winked at Nathan. "Best not t'talk to 'em. 'Especially the wimmun. You could get into trouble with 'em."

Nathan nodded. He smiled at Ellie as the soldier moved a little way away from them. "Guess I'll get me that wood!" He gave her a wave. "S'long!"

Tired though she was, Ellie returned his smile. Nathan blinked. Her expression was so pure, warm and sweet that it made his heart flip over, and he was dazzled. It sparked off a kind of electricity inside him – a warm flowing excitement. He felt he wanted to stay with her, get to know her a bit more.

But he had to move away and she didn't see him for a few minutes.

Nancy had in the meantime taken all this in, from where she

had been standing by the river bank. She'd shot Ellie a knowing look. "He likes you!"

Ellie felt the heat rush to her cheeks at this sudden revelation. She lowered her eyes bashfully. She had noticed that several of the soldiers had been watching her lately and she knew now that Nathan had been staring at her as well. She remembered that every time she'd passed him he'd smiled and winked at her. But she hadn't known his name then.

Now he was walking back her way, carrying some firewood. She jumped up, meaning to get the damp material back to the camp fire as soon as she could. But she overbalanced in her effort to get up and crashed headlong into Nathan, who promptly dropped his sticks.

"Here – steady!" His large, chunky hands were gripping her elbows. "You've bushwhacked me! Where'd you think you're going, Ellie?"

Light-headed from eating little food, Ellie smiled at him. "Sorry! My footslipped under me! Can I help you pick the branches up!"

"No need." He was so close to her, all he could think about was how much he'd like to take her in his arms and kiss her. His instinct to do that was so strong he had to clench his fists. But now wasn't the time as they were being watched by the other young soldier who was grinning nastily, so Nathan just contented himself with ruffling her jet black, thick braided hair as a goodwill gesture. "Mind yourself next time, Injun!" He tried to sound stern and failed. Ellie saw the grin in his eyes and she grinned ruefully back, her eyes sliding to the womenfolk beside the river. Nancy was regarding the proceedings with some interest.

Reluctantly, she moved away, wanting to know more about Nathan, sensing his interest in her more fully now. She wondered what it was like to kiss him, to feel those strong, manly arms around her.

A glance at Rachel's frozen face showed Ellie that the older Indian woman was not impressed with her talking to a White soldier! Ellie sighed in frustration. Her mother's shawl had fallen to the ground and looked worse than it had before! Now she would have to do the whole thing again!

<> <> <>

The old barn that the soldiers camped around was a good storage shed for the Army's provisions. It was large and airy, but it only held half of their allotted food inside it, which was a blow for the soldiers and the Indians, who soon found this out when they reached the building.

The only people to find it useful were the children, who huddled into the fresh straw, cocooning themselves with warmth from the battering wind which had mauled them upon the journey.

McGinty was angry, hungry and tired. "The Government has paid good money for those provisions!" He growled, to Sargent Mallows. "And what have I got to show for it? Nothing but oats n' coffee beans! Get me the chief bugle-boy, I've got an errand for him!"

Mallows sent word for young Jasper, who came at the run, munching cornbread. He saluted McGinty smartly.

"Yes, sir?"

McGinty eyed the cornbread hungrily. "Over the next hill, Ah d'believe ye'll find a ranch. It'll be Jesse Drew's place; here's a message for him; he's to send us the provisions stated in our agreement. Ah will not tolerate a half-share of the victuals he's left us with… Is that clear, boy?"

"Yes, sir."

"Then be off with you, double quick!"

McGinty turned to Mallows. "We'll camp here 'til the boy gets back. Give the Injuns half rations. We'll have to make do." He wanted to march off quickly to get his food.

Mallows looked worried. "Some of the Indian women won't move out of the barn, sir. They say it's too cold to come out!"

"Dammit! Well, we can't have 'em in there with the food!"

Mallows shrugged, he wanted to get his grub as well.

McGinty noticed Nathan walking by with a bucket of water. He was going to give it to the horses to drink. "Billings!"

Nathan stopped. "Yes, sir?"

"Come with me. I want those Injuns out of the barn! Bring your rifle!"

It was an order Nathan had to obey. He followed an irate McGinty into the roomy storage building.

There was quite a crowd of women in there. Some of the younger children were already asleep in the hay, and their mothers had wrapped them deeply into it.

The first person McGinty saw in there was Ellie. She glared at him as if he was the intruder and not her.

"Not you again, missy?" McGinty ignored her narrow-eyed stare.

Ellie shot a look at Nathan, then at his rifle. She didn't reply.

"Ah want all of you out of here."

Ellie found her voice: "It's too cold to be out there. Besides, many of the children are asleep now," she indicated, with a wave of her slender hand, the crowd of Indian women standing silently beside her. "Most of us are sheltering from the bad weather. It's warmer in here."

"Ah don't care if it is! You shouldn't be in here!" McGinty narrowed his eyes. He motioned to Nathan. "Remove them!"

Nathan hesitated. His eyes met Ellie's. They pleaded with her to obey McGinty. Nathan didn't want to hurt her. He didn't like this situation any more than she did.

"Ah can't have you all in here with the food! You all get out!" McGinty cried.

"We're not doing any harm! No one is going to pinch your

lousy food!" Ellie was warming up, her indignation shining through.

McGinty sighed. He strode over to her, Nathan following nervously.

"For the last time, will you get out! The children will be comfortable enough in the wagons!"

Ellie gestured with her hand outstretched again, taking in the sleeping children this time. "Even you must see that to move these children now would be very cruel... Are you a cruel man as well as a mean cussed one?"

McGinty's mouth fell open. He said, in a strangled voice: "Billings?"

"Sir!" Nathan's heart was in his throat.

"Take these women out, will you?"

"Yes, sir! What about the children, sir?"

"The children can remain here until the morning!"

Nathan breathed a sigh of relief. So did Ellie. Nathan went towards her.

"Ah'm sorry, but I got to do this!"

Ellie nodded. "At least he's allowing the children to stay!" There was an echo of triumph in her voice. She turned to the women who were gathering around her, some of them patted her admiringly on the back as they left.

It took a good half an hour before bugle-boy Jasper was back in camp. He went straight to McGinty who'd had his food and was now drinking coffee.

"Well, did you see Drew? What did he have to say for himself?"

"He wasn't at home, sir. He's had some difficulty. He's ridden off after Indians who attacked his ranch."

"What about the provisions? Are we getting anymore?"

"Ah spoke to the foreman in charge, sir, an' he said that we won't."

"Damnation! Why's that?"

"The foreman said that it was the Indians who'd taken the corn from the barn. They didn't have enough men to guard it, sir. The corn and other things can't be replaced."

McGinty blinked several times. He was really tired tonight. Not even the coffee was helping him. "Goddamn Injuns!" he growled. "If we'd arrived here on time we might have caught 'em red-handed, but we're later than Ah wanted to be – thanks to all those stops we had to make! Ah blame our Injuns for that! They are so slow!"

Jasper spoke before he could stop himself: "Walking is slow going, sir!"

McGinty shot him an irate look from under his fringe of yellow hair. He barked: "When Ah want your opinion, boy, Ah'll ask for it! Alright! Company dismissed! Let's be thankful we've been left with something – little enough as it is!"

Chapter Eight

Hard Times

At one stage upon this wild journey they entered a low canyon that filtered out onto a sliver of land that housed rocky boulders and sparse grass, but the ground was still hard with frost and chunks of snow. Here, a small wooden homestead had been left burning, acid smoke tendrils climbing into the afternoon sky, the victim of some bloodthirsty Indian attack. Since Jesse Drew had had his ranch gutted, McGinty had kept a sharp look-out for errant bands of trouble-making Indians.

Although McGinty had already seen the smoke and sent his men off ahead of his Indians to scout out the lie of the land, he wasn't totally able to stop some of the wagons entering near to the blazing cabin. One wagon did get too close, just as some burning timber smashed down beside it and the sparks flew over the cart, instantly igniting the wagon's canvas cover. It went up like lightning. Within seconds folk in the cart were running for their lives, not least the driver whose clothes were on fire.

Seeing what was happening, Frank the Preacher started to run awkwardly towards the blazing man, shouting: "Get down, brother! Roll in the snow!" He reached the Indian and pushed him to the ground, quickly taking off his own coat to wrap it around him, but McGinty got there first. He raised his rifle and held the writhing man in his gun sight.

Frank realized his intentions. "For the love of God, man – you can't shoot him!"

Frank jumped in front of the captain's horse, causing the beast to sidestep. McGinty lost his aim.

"Hog blast you, preacher!" McGinty straightened his stance and went to fire again. Something came at him with a rush and knocked him clean off his horse. The animal neighed restlessly.

Stunned, McGinty staggered up still clutching his weapon. "What the blazes?!"

Ellie was sprawled on the rough, snow encrusted ground. A pigtail had come undone. She looked like a demon from mythology with her streaked dirty face and wild, staring, accusing eyes.

"Did you just knock me down, gal?"

"I did, Tall Man!" Ellie raised herself up. Her shift had large snow-stains on it. Her blanket lay in the dirt. She had given her Indian shawl to her Mother, for warmth.

McGinty swore. He hollered: "You cussed looking hot-headed she-wolf! What are you trying t'do now?"

"Stop you from shooting that poor man!"

"We'll see about that!" McGinty went to shout for Sergeant Mallows again, but found the man was nowhere near him. So he strode straight up to Ellie, a fierce look on his face.

He slapped her face, hard. "Ah'll birch you next time, I swear!"

Tears came to Ellie's eyes as she staggered back. Seeing her stunned expression, Frank came and stood beside her, offering a steady arm for her to lean on.

"You've hit the chief's daughter – you swine!"

"Yes – and I'll hit her again if she don't behave!"

Frank said, hotly: "The chief will hear of this!"

Ellie put a hand on his arm, her left cheek stinging, turning red. "I'm alright, Frank." She pointed to the screaming Indian rolling helplessly on the ground. "But he isn't."

"No, he isn't." McGinty said grimly. He again raised his rifle and fired before either Ellie or Frank could stop him.

Ellie moaned: "No!" and she made to step towards McGinty. Frank was quick to hold her back. She struggled with him. "Let me go, Frank! He's a murderer!"

The Indian lay still and lonely in the snow, his coat charred and steaming, and his hair singed, with a single bloodshot wound to his chest.

Behind them it was still confusion as men shouted and horses neighed. McGinty mounted his horse and went off to get his troops under control, whilst Frank knelt with Ellie and the burned man's bereaved family, who had now gathered around him, and said prayers for the dead Indian.

Young as she was, Ellie found herself comforting the man's wife who was sobbing on her shoulder. "This is so awful! Cal's dead! He's dead! Yellow Beard has killed him! Why did he have to do this? Couldn't the medicine man have done something for him? Oh, dear God – my Cal!"

Frank said, soothingly: "There, there. Chief Whiteleaf will be told about this!"

"But, what can he do? Cal's dead! I'm a widow now – O Lord, help me!"

Frank glanced at a dejected Ellie and shrugged. There was nothing he could say to the woman; he had been down this road with others dying many times before on this endless walk...

He could only be there physically and spiritually for his people. That was all he could do. Sometimes, it just wasn't enough. Frank felt as low and dispirited as Ellie did.

Somehow, after nearly an hour, the whole camp managed to sort itself out and they made for flatter ground. By this time the women were shrill and sharp-tongued, flagging behind the men, weary unto death with the harsh climate and this rocky, woody country they were passing through. Even the children's eagerness had tarnished. They all walked without nourishment. Snow and rain followed them, the flakes large and so wet that they didn't set. The children's little feet left no marks on the hard, cold earth.

Chief Whiteleaf sought out McGinty. "One of my men was in an accident back there. You shot and killed him."

McGinty grimaced. "You're man was dying of third degree burns. He wouldn't have been able to continue the walk."

"You murdered him."

"Listen, old-timer! Ah did what Ah thought was best; Ah put him out of his misery."

"Then when we get to our new land, I'll report you!"

"Report away! Ah don' need any of your bellyaching! Ah was doing my job!"

"You also hit my granddaughter! Who gave you that right?"

"She was stopping me doing my job!"

"Ellie was stopping you from killing a man! Have you no compassion?"

"Sure Ah have! That Injun would have died on the road or in the back of one of those wagons at some stage or another!"

"Our medicine man would have done what he could for him. He would have freed the man's spirit without causing trauma by using the mean end of a gun – as you did!"

"You people think you know it all! Just because you live close to the earth! Spiritual crap! Well, Ah tell *you*, old-timer, Ah'm the boss around here!"

"And I'm my people's leader! If I was younger…"

McGinty sneered. "Yeah – if! Now you listen to me! That granddaughter of yours should be taught some obedience! She dang near interferes with all my plans! Keep her outa my way in future else I'll have her chained!"

Chief Whiteleaf pursed his lips in exasperation. "No one – not even you – will put chains on my granddaughter!"

But he found himself talking to the empty air. McGinty had swung away and marched off, his long yellow hair gleaming in the wintry sunlight. Chief Whiteleaf wearily shook his head in frustration. "Arrogant bastard! He should be hog tied and sent to Hell!" He muttered in Cherokee. He absent-mindedly rubbed his chest. It was hurting him again.

The entire weary settlement were glad to reach a small town later that day where they stopped again on the outskirts of the wide, mud frosted, churned-up street which wasn't so prosperous looking as Ahoamah. The few buildings that it had were widely spaced apart.

It looked like it was a lawless town as well, with no sheriff. They'd come upon a lynching.

To the right of the main saloon there was a strong tree with a rope tied securely to one of its branches, dangling in the chill wind. A hostile, angry crowd of men were gathered around an Oki Indian, who was probably from an offshoot of the Apache clan. They were trussing his arms. When Captain McGinty and some of his men rode forward into the main square, everyone turned to watch the newcomers uneasily.

The shouting and the commotion died down as if someone had shot at all the whisky bottles in the saloon.

McGinty shouted demandingly: "What's going on here?"

The men nearest to him, some dressed in cowboy gear and some in woolen suits and cowboy hats, their hands in their pockets, made way for a medium-height man who was also wearing a suit. He had an ambling gait and a sly look on his face, and he said guardedly: "Howdie. Who be you, Sirrah?!"

"Captain Rufus McGinty, 7th Infantry. What's this Indian done?"

"He stole what wasn't his. Beaver pelts. He was going t'sell 'em north o' the river."

"Them were mah pelts!" A little man wearing a beaver hat bounced into McGinty's view. "Dirty yellowsnake took 'em off mah horse in bro-oard daylight! Ah saw him!"

McGinty rested his hands on the pommel of his saddle, at ease and in control. "You aim t'lynch him for that?"

"Yessiree!" The crowd echoed the sentiment of the man with the beaver hat.

"Where's your lawman?"

"We ain't got one. He was killed 'bout two weeks ago, by another Injun from this one's tribe." It was the medium-height man who spoke up. "These Oki are always giving us trouble; time we showed them we is the boss around here!"

There was heartfelt agreement again. McGinty noticed the Indian had been strung round the neck with the rope and placed on a horse even whilst they'd been talking.

"So you want justice done? Is hanging one Indian going to cool your blood?"

The little man with the beaver hat spoke up: "Mah pelts were worth more'n 6 dollars! They wus good 'uns, and this danged Injun crawled in an took 'em, high n' mighty as yer please! Ah can't allow tha-at!"

McGinty kicked his horse and rode up to the trussed Indian. The thick crowd of men parted a little, their eyes wary and hot for action. "Is this true?"

The Indian had heavy dark eyebrows cutting across the bridge of his broad nose and a high, domed forehead. Although tied, he exuded a forceful air. He shook his head.

"Have you gotta tongue? Do you speak English?"

"Hey – Captain!" The medium-height man spoke up. "This is our party – not yours!"

"You may be right. But I represent the United States Army! I'm just making sure that justice pays."

"What's an Injun to you?" someone from the crowd shouted. A lot of folk sniggered.

McGinty shrugged. "Nothing, I've got myself my own brood!" He indicated the line of Indians and wagons behind him. He turned again to the trussed man aware that the Indians from his own group were watching the proceedings and that a weary-looking Chief Whiteleaf was now standing beside his horse. Frank the preacher man had also joined him.

McGinty again focused on the bound Indian. "You there! Is it true you stole those pelts?"

The Indian slowly shook his head, hampered by the heavy rope around his neck.

"Speak! Dammit – explain!" McGinty barked.

"They were my pelts!" The Indians voice was deep and strong. "I was claiming them back! Beaver Hat here stole them from *me* when I was out hunting!"

"My! That jus' aint true!" Beaver hat bounced into view again waving his fist. "I ketch mah own pelts; ah don' steal from no Indian!"

The bold, dark eyes of the Indian turned towards him. "You did!"

Beaver hat pointed to the Indian. "He's guilty, soldier!"

Chief Whiteleaf had been listening. He spoke up for his own kind as his people watched the scene: "I think the white trapper lies. This man does not look like a thief!"

"I agree." Frank decided. "You don' seem to have proof either way! This is barbaric! Let the man go! God would not want this to happen."

"You both keep outa this!" McGinty ordered.

Chief Whiteleaf ignored him. He asked the noose-bound Indian: "Why did he take your pelts?"

The Indian touched his left chest with a clenched right fist then drew his hand away fully flexing his fingers. Chief Whiteleaf understood the sign. "Beaver-hat! Bad trapper. Caught only 5 pelts. I catch 20! Him jealous." He then put his two index fingers together forming a cross. "I agreed to trade some pelts for firewater, but beaver-hat cheated! He took all my pelts! I came to get them back. I am no thief!"

In the background they heard Beaver-hat state his innocence. "T'aint true! I caught me them pelts fair'n'square! The Indian lies!"

McGinty rubbed his unshaven chin, shaking his head. "Ahhh! Let him go!" He turned to the medium-height man. "They're both contestin' the truth! I say: let him go!"

The medium-height man had stopped trying to look friendly. "This ain't your domain, Captain! Nor your quarrel! This Injun's for lynchin' and that's that!"

Ellie had been listening with her mother. Now she pulled Alison's skirt and whispered: "Why is Tall Man on our side, Mama? He doesn't usually take sides, does he?"

Alison shrugged, whispering back: "I don't know, Ellie. Maybe, well…maybe, he's just trying to assert himself. We women can't interfere – even for one of our own – this is men's territory! You'd best turn around, honey. This man is going to die!"

"We should stop it!"

"Now, don't you go moving off, young lady! Remember Yellow Beard's threat! He'll chain you up – he'll do it, too! Besides, there are too many Whites."

The space around McGinty's horse had suddenly thickened with determined, blood-thirsting White men intent on action – whether it was lawful or not. McGinty found he was forcefully separated from the Indian by the full force of the stubborn, surging crowd. His horse sidestepped uneasily, neighing. It forced a tight-lipped Chief Whiteleaf to move out of its way, still rubbing his chest.

McGinty conceded defeat. He saw the medium-height man raise his arm and the crowd thinned a little to allow the horse the Indian was sitting on to gallop off. His hand went down, smacked the horse's rump and the animal pulled away.

McGinty's eyes met those of the Indian whose neck, embraced by the deadly coiled rope, was feeling it draw tighter as he struggled to free himself… He uttered a cry in the thin air and strained, several times, against the tight rope, knowing that death was his companion.

Then his body jerked and swayed in the stiff breeze, his eyes closed forever on his last words. Words that could well have been true. No man was to know.

Frank bowed his head and said a prayer for him.

Chapter Nine

Ambush

As they got closer to the Mississippi River the snow turned to rain, and many wagons floundered in their tracks, which put a strain on everyone. McGinty's soldiers had to put their backs to the wagons to get them out of the mud.

The soldiers were becoming just as tired and footsore as the Indians were.

Najun found that he had the army's ailments to deal with as well as his own people.

He was with a soldier, who was having his feet seen to, when Clara came up to them.

"Najun, do you know where the chief is?"

"No."

"Oh, dear..."

"What is the matter now?"

"It's the White American woman, Kate. She and her slave, Noni, went into the woods to do the necessary, and they have disappeared!"

Najun straightened up. He said, to the soldier: "The ointment will help for a while, but I have little left; don't expect me to give you anymore."

The soldier nodded. "Ah guess Ah kin manage now... Who's gone a-missing did you say?"

Clara spoke absently. "A White woman who married into our tribe...."

Najun said: "She has Black Noni with her. She'll be alright."

The soldier nodded. Because he was a kind man and he'd become used to the Indians on this long journey he gave Najun a small wad of tobacco as thanks, and stomped off.

Clara turned to Najun. "Kate's husband is worried. She's been gone for more than an hour."

"That is bad. We must tell Yellow Beard as well as the chief!"

The pair of them went and found Ellie, who told them that her grandfather was 'resting' in one of the wagons.

Najun decided: "We won't bother the chief with this; we'll look for Kate ourselves."

"I'll come with you!" Ellie offered.

They went and found Kate's husband, Moses, and told him what they'd decided. Moses instantly brought forward some of his family who were willing to search in the rain for the missing Kate.

They went to a spot where she and her black slave had last been seen. It was a patch of dense woodland, and dark, and dreary in there.

It was Ellie who found Kate's pretty, gossamer woven shawl hanging on a tree branch.

It was drenched in blood.

"Oh no! I've found something! Over here!" she called.

They all crowded around her. Moses held his wife's shawl with a concerned look on his face. "Something has happened to Kate! We must take this to Yellow Beard!"

They searched around for a bit more, but no trace could be found of Moses's pale-haired American wife, so they trailed dispiritedly back to camp, whilst Moses and his family went to call on McGinty, who was giving orders to his men.

"She's disappeared, you say?" McGinty was only half listening; he was wondering whether to camp or not.

"She's been gone a long time." Moses answered. "I'm worried about her."

"Maybe she decided to flee? She got fed up living with y'all Injuns. She took her slave with her."

"No! She wouldn't do that – no matter how bad things became here! Look – there is blood on this shawl! I tell you something has happened to her!"

"Okay. We'll camp here. The rain is easing up." McGinty sighed. "You'd better show me where she was last seen, but Ah'm not going to waste any time on this! If she's gone she's gone!"

He took several of his men with him, whilst Moses and his family went and showed him where Kate had last been seen. They established the spot where Ellie had found the shawl.

McGinty ordered his men to scout around.

They came across an Indian feather.

At this, McGinty looked around with narrowed eyes and pursed lips. "Mallows!"

"Here, sir!"

"Ah reckon we might have unwanted company! Jesse Drew said these Injuns that attacked his ranch are Oki, an offshoot of the Apache. Ah've heard their always warring with peaceful folk. And if their roaming around here somewhere..."

"With respect, sir, it's only one feather."

"Maybe, but Ah'm not taking the chance... Tell the men to keep their eyes open! Ah want extra look-outs stationed around the camp tonight."

"What about the missing women?"

"My guess is that they've been taken. Go and tell the husband this. Ah don't think there's anything we can do t'help 'em. We'll camp awhile longer, then we'll get moving; Ah want to make it to a less exposed spot than this one!"

Mallows did as he was bid. When he was told that McGinty wasn't going to do anything to get his wife back, Moses went very quiet and thoughtful.

That night, when they camped again, Moses managed to escape the guards on duty. He crept away, in the dark, and back-tracked to the woods they'd lodged in earlier. Stealthily, with a knife he'd borrowed from a friend of the family, he prowled through the small clearing, his eyes adjusting to the dark, and looked painstakingly for any signs of other Indians.

At first, he found nothing. But once he's skirted the woods, he came across muddy prints on the ground. There was a jumble of horses' hooves as well.

It was a moonlit night and, out in the open, he could discern the signs that other people had camped here. But whether White people or Indian he wasn't sure.

Moses followed the trail they'd left, intent on getting his wife back.

If she and the servant were alive, that is.

Suddenly, he was jumped upon. He dropped his knife.

Moses grunted in surprise. He'd heard nothing! Several eager hands clamped around his arms. He was frog-marched forward. When he resisted, his capturers punched him around the face and then half-dragged him. Through a swelling eye, Moses could just make out that there were three Indians.

They led Moses towards a party of Indians, sitting on their horses, riding bareback. The upright feathers stuck in their hair were dark against the moonlight.

They dropped him to the ground. An Indian Brave seated on a piebald rode forward.

"You come from White man's camp! How many soldiers are there?"

He spoke in a dialect Moses could only just understand. Groggily, he tried to stand, but the Indians around him pushed him down again.

"What have you done with my wife?" Moses shouted.

The Indian on the horse spat on him. "How many soldiers?"

"I don't know! 200? 300? Tell me where my wife is, *please*?"

The Indian turned his horse away.

"WAIT! My wife, you son of a bitch, where is she?!"

Moses tried to get up again, the better to stop the Indian. He didn't hear or see the blow that knocked him out cold, and he didn't feel the deadly knife that entered his rib-cage...

<> <> <>

The rains had dried up for a while. It was the next morning and McGinty's camp had entered a wide open wasteland where the wagons could move easily on the blunt surface.

One of his men had reported the fact that an Indian named Moses had somehow left camp last night, and he hadn't returned. His family had become worried about him. This made McGinty uneasy. His nose scented trouble. He was just moving to the top of the line when he heard the chief bugle-boy's horn.

"Now what?" McGinty wondered.

Jasper rode up to him, swerving to a stop. He saluted hastily.

"Trouble, sir! Indians! We think there're the ones who attacked Drew's ranch! Their chasing the rearguard wagons! Look ahead – some of 'em are coming from the front! It's an ambush!"

"Crap! I was kinda expecting this to happen! Who's in charge down there?"

"Hicks an' Bushyhead, sir!"

"Go back; get them to group themselves and draw the wagons in a circle! I'll see to this end! And – boy?"

"Yes, sir?"

"Then take your horse an' ride like Hell back to that fort we passed! We may need reinforcements."

McGinty didn't wait for Jasper to register his order; he kicked his horse into action and rode to the top of the line.

"Whoa! Whoa! We've got trouble!" He shouted out to the disturbed Indians. "Circle round! Everyone to the wagons! Ah want the infantry out here an' ready to fire!"

Everyone began scurrying towards the moving wagons. The soldiers chivvied along the elderly folk, while the frightened mothers ushered their children to the safety of the big wheels.

Ellie and her family found themselves near Nathan's wagon. He gave her a broad wink as they all slid behind the canvassed cart. "Don't worry." He told a startled Ellie. "Ah've been in a situation like this before! Just keep your head down!" His rugged face was flushed red with anticipation. Not because of the killing and shooting and maiming that was due to happen, but because this ambush bought excitement to the dreary march.

Jasper, the bugle-boy had ridden quickly away as ordered. But an Indian had come out of nowhere and shot Jasper in the arm with his rifle. The boy fell off his horse in shock.

McGinty saw him fall and thought: *There goes our only hope!*

They came from the front as well as the back, just as Jasper had said, which showed how many of them there were, with war whoops that chilled Ellie's blood. They had their faces painted, their long hair tied back, showing their grim, intent, bloodthirsty eyes.

The siege had begun. Some of the soldiers carried repeater rifles. Others had to stop and jam their barrels with lead before they could fire again. Ellie saw that several of the Indians of her own clan were helping the soldiers reload their rifles and guns. She immediately tried to do the same thing, but was stopped by her mother.

"Not you! Do you want to be a target?"

"No. But I want to help!"

"You'll help by sitting still!" came the firm reply.

A haze of gun smoke soon hung over the besieged party.

McGinty had no way of knowing how the middle of his long caravan of wagons was making out. He'd assigned Sargent Mallows to this section. All McGinty could hear were the sounds of rifles and guns going off somewhere in the far distance.

As far as he knew he only had about 85 men up the front with him. Going by the Oki milling around them, they were outnumbered.

He was using his Colt for a clearer, steadier shot. He shot an

Indian Brave that was attempting to make his pony jump the traces of a wagon. The horse thundered away, riderless.

Women and children squealed as the sounds of battle reached a crescendo. Ellie's mother covered her ears with her hands, flinching away from the shots.

Another Indian had made it to their territory. Nathan saw him. His own rifle had jammed, so he got out his hunting knife, ready to defend the womenfolk.

He swung at the Indian who sidestepped smartly, and brought his knife down, hacking at Nathan's wrist. Nathan moved back, and then surged forward, so that it was the Indian's turn to twist away and come up underneath Nathan's lunge.

He caught Nathan, nicking him in the arm and drew blood. Nathan didn't even notice, he was so intent on his persecutor.

As the Indian lunged again with another uppercut, Nathan kicked out. The knife flew from the Indian's hand. Nathan jumped him. They both struggled desperately, but Nathan had his weight to steady him. He mercilessly plunged his knife into the Indian's body. He landed with a thud beside a frightened Ellie, dead.

As some of the soldiers fell, Ellie's tribe immediately took the rifles and began shooting too. McGinty was too busy to notice. But after what seemed like a long time he did hear a familiar sound...

It was the noise of a bugle! The army was coming!

There was ragged cheering from McGinty's men. Hearing the bugle, the Indians, who had all but surrounded the first 25 wagons, pulled out of the affray sharply, wheeling their horses away from battle, their victorious voices stilled at this new menace that was coming in their direction.

With guns primed and ready to defend the 2nd Reserve Battalion rode hell for leather towards the wagons, whilst several groups of soldiers on horseback swept after the errant Indian Braves.

"Yahoo! Give 'em Jesse!" McGinty's soldiers yelled, standing atop the seats on some of the wagons.

Riding along with the battalion was a jubilant Jasper. He had blood all over his arm, but the injury had been roughly bandaged. The boy had managed to crawl away in the skirmish and get help after all!

It took McGinty and his soldiers most of the day to sort out the dead and injured. The 2nd Reserve Battalion had brought bandages with them and other first aid paraphernalia, so Najan and the camp doctor from the Battalion were busy seeing to injuries.

Nathan had allowed his hand to be bandaged. "Someone else will have to feed an' water the horses," he said, matter-of-factly.

One of the soldier's that had been injured had been Bill Hicks, but he made no complaint when Najun bandaged his burly chest after they'd got out a bullet that had been meant for the big man's heart.

"A've got nine lives!" he joked, tapping his torso proudly.

"Maybe. But you could have caught pneumonia the other night when you gave your coat to that sick child!" Najun scolded.

"Is the child alright now?" Bill asked.

Najun didn't meet his eyes. Bill took one look at him and groaned. "Ah take that as a 'no'" he said, softly.

Najun nodded mournfully. "I'm sorry."

The mature soldier merely replied: "It's this darn walk! It should never have been allowed! McGinty's a fool – he's movin' us on too fast!"

"Yellow Beard is too impatient!" Najun agreed. He glanced up from his bandaging. "Here comes a friend of yours."

It was Nathan. He squatted down beside Bill. "How are ye doing?"

"Stiff and sore, but I'll live! See you got a bandage on?"

"It's nothing - compared with what we lost."

"How many?"

"About Fifty. Their still countin' 'em. They got Claymure and Compton, I'm afraid."

"They were my best pals!"

"Ah'm sorry, Bill. But you still got me! Ah'm a best pal, too, aren't I?"

"You bet, Nathan! You know....when Ah'm better, Ah'm going to take French leave....Ah'm going to get me to South Dakota, I've a squaw there, runs by the name of Rising Moon. She sure is pretty, an' Ah miss her!"

Nathan grinned. "Your're a dark horse, Bill!"

"You're welcome to come with me!"

"Ah'm thinking A'll stay here awhile. There's someone here Ah'm interested in."

"Wouldn't be the Chief's granddaughter, would it?"

Nathan sighed. "You know too much, Bill! Ah'll come back to help you up when you've rested awhile..... See you later!"

Bill winked at Najun. "He's a good boy."

Najun didn't reply.

Chapter Ten

River Crossing

They'd come by wagon and foot, now they were to cross the Mississippi River which was at least three quarters of a mile wide and filled with fast-moving ice floes and dislodged trees. It was mid-December and bitingly cold and Ellie's group had made better time than some of the other groups, who would not make the crossing until January.

It was now impossible to travel along the roads towards the Mississippi river due to the mud that the next heavy winter rains had made. This happened shortly after the Oki had been warned off attacking McGinty's cavalcade. The wagons just couldn't move.

Sergeant Mallows spoke to McGinty: "There's a hardware store ahead, sir. We're going to need heavy boards, extra heavy duty chains, bolts n' nails."

"Ah figured that out, Mallows," McGinty snapped. "Ah'll go an' have a word with the shopkeeper!"

He stomped inside the store whose shelves were laden with hardware. The shopkeeper, a round barrel of a man, greeted him warmly enough. McGinty requested what he wanted.

"That'll be two and a quarter thousand dollars!" The shopkeeper told him, grinning broadly.

"Two and a quarter thousand dollars! I haven't got two and a quarter thousand dollars, man!"

The shopkeeper's amiability faded. "Then ah can't help you, sir."

"Look – Ah'll give ye one an' a half thousand. Will that do?"

"No, sir, it won't."

"Then I'll take my custom elsewhere." McGinty decided, stubbornly.

The shopkeeper cleared his throat, looking modest. "I think you'll find we are the only timber store for miles around. There ain't many stores like mine that kin offer you good value for money!"

McGinty could see the man had him where he wanted him. He was desperate to get across the Mississippi and the storekeeper knew it, going by his smug smile.

The storekeeper said now: "I can give you a good bargain offer, sir. How's about we say a round two thousand dollars – for all that you need?!"

"You're a hard man, mister." But McGinty was swayed. He had to make a fast decision. "Two thousand it is then. Done!" he said, "an' not a cent more!"

He'd got his boards and heavy duty chains, but at a price.

If the hard ground by the Mississippi wasn't worse enough, there was a real scarcity of grazing land and game which further hit the infants, the young and the elderly.

In the words of one Cherokee, speaking to Frank: "We have to cut through the ice to get water for ourselves and the animals. It snows every two or three days and the mud is hard. Our wagons flounder. We keep going west. Many days pass and many die very much. I have never experienced such cold weather before."

This was true of the river crossing. The middle of winter was on them as they halted beside the river, with hundreds of sick and dying penned up in wagons, or stretched out upon the ground with only a blanket to keep out the icy chill.

Many Indians died huddled together at Mantle Rock as they waited to cross. Some groups crossed at Cape Girardeau, Missouri, although many townsfolk did not like this idea. They were against the rows of Indians camping near their town. Several Indians were charged a dollar a head to cross the river.

They all had to settle beside the river, many dying of dysentery. The Muskogee Creek Indians called the Mississippi River the Wewogufkee Thakko (Big Muddy Water). Manyof the boats on the raging river were old and dilapidated and didn't look strong enough to carry armloads of passengers across to the other side.

Several Cherokee groups were waiting to cross the Mississippi, but the river levels were too low for navigation. There were instances where those who did manage to board a barge got hit by dangerous ice floes and the barges sank and the people drowned.

One such family was Elijah's. The Cherokee was busy placing his wife and children onboard a dilapidated keel boat. His wife caught him by the shoulder just as he was about to go. Her shawl was soaked with river spray and she and the children were shivering.

"You are not coming over with us, husband?"

"I must go back for Uncle. We will meet on the next crossing, Sarah."

She relented grudgingly, and held out her arms for Elijah to hand her their baby boy.

"Let me have Ben, then. But hurry to us soon. *Soon*! You hear, husband mine! We can't be without you!"

"I promise." Elijah held her to him briefly and then moved away, tripping through the ice crusted mud that lined the Mississippi's banks.

The old keel boat sloughed off into the rapid river like a tipsy maiden, boards creaking under its heavy load of people. Sarah tried to wave from the rails but her baby was too heavy a burden to hold onto. Her little girl, Polly, waved for her.

Then the unspeakable happened. It had begun to rain heavily. Torrents of wet, icy rain whipped the fragile craft, as the boat's Captain jerked the massive pilot wheel to avoid ram-roading trees. A huge piece of ice crunched into the boat broadside on.

She keeled to straight away sending many of those standing near the rails into the swirling, raging water. Tipped in amongst them was Sarah, her baby and Polly.

Those on the bank shouted a warning. Elijah stumbled over to the water's edge, his mouth open in shock and horror.

"Sarah! Sarah, my darling! I'm coming!" Dragging off his ragged Sunday-best coat he plunged headlong into the icy river before anyone could stop him.

Those on the bank that awful day saw Elijah swim towards the stricken keel boat. Others were already diving in to save their loved ones, but the fast flowing current was against all of them. It was too strong. In the threshing, muddy water, splashing bodies struggled past, calling for help.

Those whom the current had pulled into shallower waters were luckier than Elijah's family for they were able to be dragged out, whey-faced and exhausted from their ordeal.

But Elijah couldn't see his family, blinded as he was by the tumbling, swirling water. He dived again and again looking for them. He swam until he could no longer swim; exhausted and shaking with the cold, but he couldn't locate his family. They'd gone, been cruelly swept away by the force of the tumultuous waters.

He finally dragged himself towards shallow water, his face stiff and cold in shock, quivering in every limb with his exertions, and that was where Martha found him. Without a word, she pulled his hand roughly into her own and led the stricken man back to one of the camp fires that had been set up beside the water's edge.

"You poor man! You come with me," she said. No one could offer him any solace. He lived in his own hell. So much so that he was unaware of her solicitous help as she roughly chaffed his cold hands.

"My family! I can't believe…" He buried his face in his hands, sobbing out his anguish.

Martha saw there was coffee on the camp fire. Since this trip, many Indian families had learnt how to make the coffee that the soldiers provided them with. She poured some out for herself and Elijah.

"Here – drink this."

The man's hands were trembling so much he could hardly hold his tin cup. Martha assisted him, gently forcing him to drink the scalding liquid. He was like a child in her hands. She asked: "Have you relatives who will take care of you?"

"There's Uncle… (I'd forgotten about him)… All I could think about was to save my family! But I am alive and they are dead! I am a wretched, selfish man…why couldn't I have died with them! My wife wanted me to come aboard with her! I wish I had now!"

"Hush! Don't take on so. It is YellowBeard's fault – forcing us to cross this dangerous river! Now, tell me your uncle's name and I will see if I can find him for you."

She called around for those nearby to help her, and because she was the chief's wife, she got the help she needed. Within three hours Elijah had been reunited with his uncle.

When Chief Whiteleaf heard what she had done he gave his wife the best accolade that he could. He told her: "You are the highest of women, Martha. I am proud to be your husband!"

"Then stop rubbing your chest so often! Does it hurt you there?"

"No. No! No! I am alright, my love! Don't worry about me!" He was so insistent that Martha put it out of her mind. She was to remember it later.

Others drowned that day as well. One of them was Frank.

It wasn't his turn to board the ferry; he was at the end of one long queue, Ellie and Alison at the front.

"Roll aboard there!" A ferryman beckoned to Ellie. She jumped onto the plank and in two strides was on the tossing raft. Alison made to follow, but the ferryman stopped her. "Cant y'see? We're full! Wait for the next ferry!"

Ellie's eyes snapped open in sudden distress as Alison said: "There's room for me, isn't there? I have to be with my daughter!"

"Sorry! Can't do!"

Ellie cried out amidst the noise of the foaming water: "WAIT! I'm not going without my ma!"

"Then get back t'her! Ah can't take both of you!"

"Come back, Ellie!" her mother called. "We'll travel on the next ferry!"

Ellie did as she was told.

"Room f'one more!" The boatman hollered. "Anybody!"

Of all the groups nearby no one wanted to be separated from their friends and relatives. The boatman spotted Frank. "You on your own there! You wanna hop on, preacher? I got me some room here!"

Frank looked around him. "Okay!" he decided, and strode aboard.

It was the last time Ellie and her mother saw him.

The ferry moved out into the Mississippi.

It was still rough. Ice floes, sharp, cold and dangerous streamed rapidly by. The little ferry was crowded with Indians clutching their shawls around them, heads bent against the miserly wind.

Frank was in the middle of the ferry, holding a baby for a mother who was trying to adjust her shawl the better for carrying her child with.

The ice floe struck the ferry at the midsection, instantly pushing it further into the middle of the river with its force and snapping it in half. People toppled over the sides at the impact, including Frank, still holding the baby.

The savage cold of the steely river gripped his body even as he sank into the bubbling wet water, the weight of it pushing him, rolling, threshing, tumbling down, down, down…

The shock of the ascent numbed him. He'd let go of the baby in the sudden impact of hitting the water and with his arms flailing in all directions, he was momentarily helpless to grab hold of the infant against the might of the raging river and the pressure of the water's weight around his body enclosing him in it's cruel, death-hugging kiss.

He kicked hard to try to raise himself up, but the river held him in its relentless grip and a particularly jagged shard of ice hit the back of his head. Blood oozed from the cut and he began to feel light-headed, gasping for air. His lungs filled with the searing cold water. He gave up the ghost, drowning in shallow water, but not near enough to all those anxiously watching, waiting to drag his sodden body out. No one could rescue the baby either. Its small body was dragged and tossed downstream never to be seen again. The baby's mother drowned as well. Most of the Indians on that crossing were Cherokee from Ellie's village and the baby had been born before the march started. It was only over three month's old.

Someone in the crowd said: "They have all gone!" and Ellie shivered anew at the tragedy; she had nearly stepped onto that ferry.

Chief Whiteleaf died of a heart attack. The pain in his chest had reached a climax and he had not told even his wife that he was being troubled by illness, so as not to worry her, even though she'd noticed that something was wrong.

His had been amongst the deaths they endured when Ellie and Alison's party eventually reached snowy land the other side of the Mississippi. Those who had made it to the other side had to wait for fresh wagon relays to arrive. A lot of camping gear got lost in the swirling waters when the boats sunk. With hindsight, McGinty had sent scouts over the Mississippi before the Indians embarked onto the boats. These scouts had gone on ahead to commission more Government wagons to replace those that couldn't make the water crossing, which was nearly all of them.

Ellie had come back from washing her face in an ice-laden creek they were passing one frosty morning. No matter how often she washed her face, it always got dirty again in the cold grey environment that they were passing through.

She came upon a circle of soldiers and Indians standing with hands on hips, staring down at the snow-kissed, frozen ground. Alison was bending down holding someone's hand. There was a lot of low murmuring going on, and Ellie pushed her way forward, wondering what had happened now.

As she neared the center of the group her mother's cold dark eyes swept towards her, her face full of tears for Chief Whiteleaf. In one glance Ellie could see the old chief lying like a fallen bear on the snow-encrusted ground, his Bandera that he had worn around his head knocked askew and his face grimacing back at her in a death mask of agony. His wife was flung, full-stretch over his body, moaning bitterly, her grey hair in disarray, her knotted, bony hands clutching his once warm blanket and jacket so tightly that her knuckles glared white.

"I think his heart gave out," someone muttered to someone else. "Couldn't take the God-awful strain anymore, he couldn't. Went down like a deer stumbling over a rock."

Around Ellie the women of the tribe were moaning sorrow-fully in mournful tones, their blistered and dirty hands covering their haunted, haggard shawl-covered faces, hiding their tears.

Ellie's mother was sobbing quietly, her worn hands covering her eyes, her shoulders shaking with emotion. Ellie urgently pushed past her and dropped down beside her grandmother. "E-ni-si? What has happened to Grandfather? Why is he lying down like that?"

Her grandmother looked at her with eyes that were raw and red-rimmed. "Because he can't get up...ever again... Oh, Ellie, dearest, you must be brave. Your grandfather is dead! He has gone to where the eagles soar!"

"Oh, no! Please tell me he's not dead! Not my E-du-di!"

Ellie's grandmother nodded, dully.

"Oh, no!" Ellie moaned again. "Not Grandfather! Oh, it's so unfair! He wanted to walk all the way with us!" She began to cry, turning away from the stiff figure lying in the snow, towards Alison, who was also still weeping. The pair hugged each other tightly in grief.

Martha narrowed her eyes. She placed a hand over her grand-child's. She said: "His spirit will walk with us. I know this. Take heart, child." She had gathered her composure again. She was once more the chieftain's wife. Alison and Ellie helped her to stand up. When she did, she hugged first Ellie, then her daughter as they stood in a solemn circle around the old chief's body.

Najun had also been kneeling beside the chief. He closed the chief's eyes gently, with great respect. "His soul left too quickly for me to fetch his spirit animal that would guide him to the happy hunting ground. There is nothing I can do here. I am very, very sorry. I can still dance for him if you want me to."

Matha blinked tiredly. She put a hand on his arm. "Wado, Najun. I don't think that is necessary."

Their chief had meant a lot to them and the clan wept for him for days after they buried him, their hearts full of pain, their souls buried beneath the avalanche of grief that now seemed to pour down upon them.

Martha begged McGinty to be left behind with her husband. He let her have her way. What was one more Indian anyway? He had his hands full, trying to feed the living thanks to the measly allowance the Government had given him, let alone bury the dead properly.

When she heard that this was Martha's wish, Clara went at once to the old chieftain's wife. She had wanted to go and hold council with Alison, but Alison was not well and had made it clear she did not want to be approached. Curiously – probably because she had married a half-blood – Alison was not so close to her mother as she had been to Chief Whiteleaf.

Clara spoke persuasively and animatedly to Martha, saying heatedly: "You are part of us. You must stay! In your time maybe, it was custom to lie with the dead! But this is different now – we cannot lose our mother on this walk as well as our father! You must have heart to journey on! I and the others, we will help you!"

Martha looked very old and shrunken, even though her large girth was well-padded in her covering of shawls. Her eyes were dull and downcast and her breath steamed on the wind when she spoke: "Daughter. I thank you, but my place is with my husband."

"No! It isn't!" Clara was determined. She held up her hands to the growling sky and her shawl slipped down revealing her own gnarled, capable, wrinkled, brown arms.

"I appeal to you to stay with us! You are our mother. We cannot let you go!"

"You will survive without me."

"Not so! You are our survival! More so now that the chief has gone, we need you! Your granddaughter needs you!"

"Don't bring Ellie into this!"

"But it isn't your time to go! I beg of you to think what this will do to your granddaughter if you leave us now!"

Martha shuddered. She turned her back for a moment, her eyes hooded and thoughtful. "I cannot betray my husband."

"But you'd be betraying us – your people! You do not deserve to die upon a stone-covered mound, stiff and cold with only the snow as a shroud upon you in this wasteland of ice! So – come with us! Come! Come!"

Martha's eyes, that had seen a lifetime flow by, surveyed the camp and her people. A few tears squeezed their way down the seamed, noble Indian woman's broad face.

Clara waited anxiously, arms folded again inside her shawl. Then she had an idea; she called to Ellie who was passing.

"Child! Come to your grandmother!"

Ellie instantly obeyed, her big bold eyes glancing from Martha to Clara, sensing the tension between the women and wondering what it was all about.

Clara pulled the girl towards her and fastened her cold hands on Ellie's shoulders.

"Would you really have the heart to leave this one? This child is your sunshine!" she challenged.

Martha looked fondly at her granddaughter. She held out her arms and Ellie found herself pushed into them and held passionately with great love.

"E-ne-si?" she murmured, wondering what was wanted of her.

"You're grandmama is thinking of leaving us." Clara spoke flatly.

Ellie understood. Instantly, she tightened her grip around her grandmother's ample waist. "No! E-ni-si! You can't do that! I love you too much to let you go!"

Martha cleared her throat. She looked away, feeling the pressure of her grandchild's body against hers, and the heavy burden of her choice. "You must stay with your mother, Ellie, my dearest. Look after her for me!"

"But you must stay, too! You are our strength, Grandmama! Without you, we are lost. You *must* stay!" A sudden thought entered Ellie's head and she looked up at her grandma and said, boldly: "Grandpapa would not want you to leave us. I know this here!" She struck her chest twice.

Clara nodded emphatically. "You're granddaughter speaks true, Martha! Listen to her! Listen to us!"

They both waited anxiously. Martha looked as if she was

going to choke.

"Child!" She hugged Ellie, shaking her head. Then she looked up at Clara. "Alright, I stay! But that man – that chief soldier, Yellow Beard. Him I do not like. Him I would not stay for!"

<> <> <>

The dreary march had begun to affect Ellie now. Back in Ahoama she'd played with the other Indian girls and had helped her mother with exquisite beadwork, stitching and sewing garments together, which she'd liked doing best. She had sometimes been allowed to follow the men when they'd gone trapping for beaver pelts.

Alison was always asking Ellie to help her with her chores, but the young girl's mind was quick and alert and she didn't want to be tied down doing what Alison did all day, she wanted adventure; to go with the men and boys and watch them hunt. She weaved her own dreams and desires of what her life might hold in store for her, once she'd left school, which had only been earlier that year. Somewhere in the future, she'd dreamed of marriage, having a husband, a family. But not yet, she told herself, not just yet. There had been boys around her, but she hadn't fallen in love with any of them. She wondered to herself what falling in love meant. What was it like? She was curious. She constantly thought of Nathan, the thickset man with the chunky, grinning face and strangely alluring masculinity.

At night, when she and her mother had visited the town square, she'd listened sleepily to the elders as they smoked their pipes, telling bold tales of ancient battles, weaving stories of myths and legends with true facts that fascinated the young girl's ears.

No one told stories anymore. Those elders she knew who were surviving were crippled with the walk, backs bent in mindless anguish, automatically pushing themselves forward, saving even their words for fear they'd lose strength.

People lost their strength every day of the walk, someone new succumbed to the agony of this monotonous march. Even Ellie's mother fell ill – more from exhaustion than anything else.

It was Ellie who was nearest to her mother when Alison unexpectedly swayed sideways beside her as they were climbing along a particularly awkward stretch of track.

"E-tsu!" Ellie immediately shot out an arm to steady her mother. "What is wrong?"

Alison panted. She shook her head wearily. "I feel faint. I must rest!"

Ellie glanced at the straggling set of Indians passing them. "I'll help you, Mama. You can rest when we get to the bottom of this track. Just keep going a bit further, please!"

Alison shook her head, wearily. "I can't go on."

"You must try! Look, I'll help you over this stony bit… See – there isn't too far to go!"

Alison stopped. She was trembling with the effort of walking any further. "Ellie, my sunshine, you must go on without me – I'll catch you up!"

"Oh no, Mama – I'm not leaving you here!"

Alison tried to offer a reassuring smile, but it came out as a grimace. "I'll be alright. Go on, Ellie. Remember – I love you!"

Easy tears came to Ellie's eyes, desperate now, she grabbed her mother's arm, and pulled. "I can't leave you here! What am I going to do without you?"

But Alison had slithered to the ground. Her eyes were closed. Ellie shook her. To her horror her mother did not open her eyes. She had fainted away as quickly as if someone had thrown a stone at her, knocking her down.

"E-tsu!" Ellie's shocked shout halted the column of straggling walkers beside her. They stood and stared hopelessly at Ellie and Alison, shuffling their feet listlessly, too exhausted to help.

McGinty rode up. He seemed to have more energy than any of

them, even though his cold eyes looked tired. "Move on – we've got a day's journey to cover!"

Ellie had knelt beside her mother, wondering desperately how she could help her. At the captain's words indignation and anger swept through her, her face contorted into a look of rage as much as the old Indian chief's had done when he'd died, she shrieked out: "Stop pushing us on you lousy beast! Can't you see there's something wrong with Mama!"

"Ah see that she's ill," McGinty said. "We'll have to leave her here!"

"You can't!"

McGinty glanced down at her from his horse. His stern gaze did not soften. "We have to push on. The longer we stay out in this weather the worse our chances of survival! Ah can't stop just for one woman – even if she is your mother! Ah could shoot her where she lies if Ah had to – if she don't get up!"

Ellie gaped at him, round-eyed.

"You wouldn't dare!"

McGinty's cold green eyes regarded her haughtily and the blond man's lips smirked down at her.

"None of you care, do you?" The words spurted from her chapped lips in a disconsolate wail and was left to flutter in the cold air like butterfly wings flapping in space.

To her surprise McGinty swung down off his horse and crouched beside her. His eyes on Ellie's agonized face he listened against Alison's chest to see if he could hear a heartbeat. He did.

"She's fainted, that's all." He took hold of Ellie's wrist and dragged the girl up with him.

He gave her a slight shake. "Now, no more hysterics, Ellie. See? Your friends are bringing a cradle for your mam, as there's no more room in the wagons!"

It was true. A rough cradle made of bark, which the Indians had used before, had appeared as if by magic out of the back of one of the wagons. Ellie saw, through a mist of tears, that some of the Indians had come forward, ready to help lift up her mother, and she was grateful to them.

"Wado!"

They acknowledged her thanks. Ellie turned again to McGinty. "She wouldn't have fainted if you hadn't pushed us on so hard!"

McGinty turned from her anguish, not bothering to reply as he remounted his horse and trotted away.

Ellie put her hands to her face, disconsolate, empty with hunger. She swayed in shock.

Martha came to her and held Ellie in her arms for a moment, steadying the stunned girl.

"I thought this was going to happen," she said. "I could see how tired she was getting."

Nancy and Clara also came by and hugged Ellie. After a moment's silence, as Martha stared after her collapsed and exhausted daughter, she motioned that Ellie should follow her. Ellie stumbled after her with tears in her eyes. She felt the cruel cold tighten around her with the knowledge that her mother was no longer at her side to support her, and she realized how much she had relied upon Alison.

As the days passed she tried to nurse Alison in her own haphazard way, sometimes being helped by the other women including her grandmother and Clara, sometimes alone, finding a loving moment to cradle her mother's dark coiled head in her lap, always wishing desperately that she had more wraps, or some thicker kind of blanket that she could cover her mother with. But Alison never opened her eyes.

The soil around them was getting lighter and less stony. In her misery and anxiety over her mother's health Ellie didn't notice. She had no idea where they were now. She only knew that they had covered many miles and that there were other miles to go.

With Alison ill, she had begun to hate the journey even more than she hated the cold.

Chapter Eleven

Loss

Familiar faces – so many had gone. Ellie still had her sick mother. She was full of fear for her mother's welfare, as well as her own. Every day, the jolting stretcher ride took more and more out of the destitute Alison, as if some whirlpool of energy was sucking out the very dregs of her mother's soul. Ellie had become very worried.

She spoke to Martha whose wise counsel she trusted both as her grandmother and as her friend. "Why can't Mama wake up? She has no fever, so what is wrong with her?"

Martha had stared up at the moon, for they were camping at night under a starlit open sky that for once was not heavy with snowfall. "She is tired. Since your pa died she has been tired in spirit as well as in body."

"But that was last year!"

"Loss can take many years to overcome, child. You will understand that, one day."

Martha looked down into Ellie's eyes. There was desperation and uncertainty in them as Ellie wailed: "Is Mama going to die!"

Her grandmother sighed heavily and cuddled the girl closer to her. "I hope not, child. I hope not. You are both so dear to me! But your mother is disenchanted with this walk. She has allowed herself to become downhearted and feeble—"

"She misses Ahoamah! So do I!"

"We all miss Ahoamah – the good, Georgia soil! This promise of a fresh start in a new land, I doubt I will ever get used to it! We're being forced to go where we don't want to live! I am too old for it!"

"Oh, E-ni-si," Ellie groaned in alarm, but her grandmamma spoke on as if she hadn't heard her.

"And with your grandfather gone, even though I am sure that we will meet our ancestors again in the other world, I am cut in half. I mourn every day for that which I have lost, and for that which I may lose again." She spoke with ice in her voice.

Fear clutched Ellie's heart. "What do you mean, E-ni-si? I miss Grandpapa too, but you are talking funny!"

Ellie's grandmother's eyes closed for a moment. "Then forget what I just said. It will be the will of the Sky God if your mother regains consciousness. She is so weak from hunger! We can get no goodness into her while she sleeps! We must wait. I see clouds on the pathway that we travel. I can offer no comfort, child, except to say that I dearly love you."

Ellie answered from her heart, passionately and fiercely. "I love you too, E-ni-si."

At her grandchild's words, Martha gave Ellie a long, hard hug. They were silent for a while. Martha's mood had changed to one of reminiscence. "Do you remember that dog you had once?

Ellie was startled. "Pinto? Oh, yes! He was one crazy dog! He used to snap at the horses hooves and make all the horses skitter about as they tried to get out of his way!"

Martha smiled. "Do you remember that time he ate all the cake? We knew he'd eaten it because of the flour left on his nose!"

Ellie's mood lightened. She chuckled. "He slunk away with his tail between his legs! Fancy you thinking of that, E-ni-si!"

Martha nodded. She held Ellie tighter to her. "They were good days... Perhaps, in time to come, we'll have other good days again!"

"I'll pray for that!" Ellie said earnestly. She added, after a moment: "It is good of you to think of the old times... You are trying to cheer me up, aren't you, like you used to do when I was very little? That was when Mama was well—" Her voice thickened with unshed tears. "Oh, Gran'mama! It seems to me as if life has stopped for us. I can't explain what I mean, but—"

"Oh, I understand exactly! We keep walking in circles in this barren land, and it seems we are getting nowhere! Every day, we are caught in the same endless nightmare."

"I know; this walk is driving me mad! Will it ever end?"

"Yes. It has to. We have to go on. We'll have Ahoama in our hearts – wherever we go. That is our only comfort, child."

"You know what would offer me the greatest comfort now – apart from you, E-ni-si?"

"No?"

"To see Mama wake up."

"Oh yes, yes." Martha sighed. There were unshed tears in her eyes now too. "We both want that to happen very much indeed."

"I am so tired of this endless walking! It goes on and on!"

"And I. My bones are too old for it! But we must go on. We can't go back. Not now."

"But it is so cold and…lonely out here. When we lived in Ahoama, we had a community! We had our lives, and we had sunshiney days… The soldiers destroyed all that! It is all gone!"

"I prefer to remember Ahoama as it was, not what it was like the day the soldiers came, spoiling everything and desecrating our homes! The White people even robbed our corpses of their jewelry and rings!"

"That is true… It's not fair!" Ellie suddenly exploded. "Bad things are happening to us every day. But I don't want to think about anything bad, like leaving Ahoama, and Mama being ill, or I'll cry! I am going to cry anyway, for I miss those good times very much!" She began to weep, from exhaustion, from hunger, from loss. She sobbed with her grandmother for her mother's health, joining her tears with the rest of a proud nation that had lost so much.

Later that evening, she took leave of her grandmother and wandered back to the flowing river, her eyes still red from sobbing. She hoped that walking beside the river would give her solace. She chose to sit on a hard rock – and solace came.

Nathan hunkered towards her, whistling along the track. He

stopped when he saw her, head hung low, disconsolate.

"Hallo! What's up? It's Ellie, isn't it?"

Ellie hung her head, looking away, her long dark hair blowing softly over her face as she did so. She combed her hair back away from her face absently, her sorrowful eyes resting on the dark, glossy swirling water of the swift flowing river beside her.

"What's up? Things ain't so dandy for you?" Nathan repeated, squatting down beside her tense body, wanting at once to offer her some comfort.

"There is something wrong with my mother. I am so frightened, full of foreboding for her!"

Hesitantly, because he didn't know her that well, Nathan lightly touched her shoulder.

"If there is anything Ah can do to help, tell me."

She felt the touch. It gave her reassurance in a time where reassurance seemed impossible. She said: "Wado." Then she added, as an afterthought: "I don't suppose you could get another blanket? It's not for me – it's for my mother!"

"A blanket? Sure thing! Stay there, Ellie, an' I'll go an' git one!"

He was as true as his word, even although she had to wait quite a while for it. There were many wagons, and it had taken Nathan some time to find the one that housed the bedding and stuff. He lumped it over to her, a huge grin on his open, chunky face.

"Got one! Here – you think this will be alright for your mam?"

"Oh, I'm so pleased with it! Wado! Wado! Wado!" She almost hugged him.

"Steady on! It's only a blanket!"

"Oh, but you don't know how much this means for me, to know that my mother will be just that bit warmer tonight, thanks to you! Maybe it will help her to wake up and eat something. She needs to – badly."

"That's good, Ah guess… Ah hope she's better soon! Well – be seeing you, Injun! Mind how you go with that blanket!"

"I will!" She wanted to blow him a kiss. Instead, she settled for a wave as she left him, feeling so much happier than she had done.

But in the early hours of a frost-kissed morning, her mother died without regaining consciousness.

Ellie had eaten very little and she was dog-tired from lack of sleep, her feet aching with the cold and from the endless walking. She was in a semi-stupor herself, her eyes heavy, and all she wanted to do was sleep now. But she kept vigil beside Alison, checking to watch that olive-colored, weary face for signs of recovery. Shadowy figures of her tribe shuffled around her as she tried to rest, her face in her arms.

Later, she was surprised awake by Nathan passing by. "Don't forget to have something to eat later, won't you? Ah know it won't be much, but..."

She was comforted by his quiet attention and still grateful to him, as she turned once again, to check on her mother.

There was a stillness about that known face that caught her attention; Alison looked the same, but different. Alerted by some foreknowledge beyond her understanding, Ellie leaned over her mother, her hand hovering in mid-air, struck by a difference in her mother's features that she couldn't fathom...

Nathan had also sensed something. Ellie heard him kneel beside her. She looked at him questionably, her mouth open.

Nathan shook his head. He put his ear to Alison's chest, listened, then picked up the woman's listless hand and checked her wrist. He was frowning.

"Mighty silly of me... Maybe A'm not doing this right, but Ah can't get a pulse!"

Ellie swallowed. She felt panicky and sprung up, making Nathan glance at her sharply. "What can we do? Help her!"

She glanced desperately at the other groups of tired Indians sitting around her, wishing someone would come forward and offer their assistance. But all the groups were asleep around separate fires, all absorbed in their world of dreams – their only escape from this harsh reality.

Ellie grabbed Nathan's shoulders and shook him. "Something's happening to her! *Do something!*"

Nathan looked both startled and grim. "Ah can't."

Ellie fell to the ground, gashing her knee sharply on a stone. Blood oozed out, but she didn't notice. She watched her mother's face. It was empty of expression, as if all life had faded from it.

The fresh morning's milky sky glimmered frostily, and the dawning day was hushed and still. Beside her, Ellie heard Nathan say: "Sorry, Ellie. Ah think your ma has gone."

The breath was knocked out of her. This walk had swallowed Alison's soul. She felt the cold even more then. It passed through every inch of her young body. She sank over that beloved figure, a wail of anguish slicing through her throat, not even noticing that Clara, Martha and Nancy had woken at her call. With fatigue in their hearts they pressed close to her to offer her their sisterly comfort.

Chapter Twelve

A Friend in Need

The days that passed where like living in a whirlpool. Ellie had no notion of the passing hours. She was stuck in a grief-stricken daze where time seemed to hang suspended in every direction.

Her loss seemed too hard to bear. Men and women of her clan moved in front of her, dragging their footsteps, and she saw them all in a shocked haze, as they buried her mother, adding their hungry sorrows to her sorrows, like a line of socks hanging up, drifting sorrowfully in the breeze.

She received all their attention, stiff and absolute, in the same imperious way that her grandmother did, the fire of life lying shallow within her heart. Nothing, *nothing* could be worse than this!

Under the shadow of her mother's love Ellie had had security of a caring kind. Now that was all gone and the girl was undone and distraught, feeling alone even though she had other women around her.

Nathan kept visiting her and she allowed it because he seemed to understand what she was going through.

"My mam died when Ah was young. Ah must have been about six at the time... Ah had no one t'care for me 'cept my old gran'pa, who Ah lived with for some years. Then Ah upped and joined the army."

"What about you're pa?"

"He lit out when Ah was born. He couldn't stand the crying, Ah guess."

"Don't you miss your ma – I miss mine all the time. I keep expecting her to come up and hug me, like she used to do... I miss her so very, very much!"

"Ah know you do. It's hard, isn't it? Yep. Ah did miss her –

usually when Ah fell over and hurt myself! But now Ah'm in the army Ah can remember her with a warm glow in my heart!"

"I don't have any warmth in me! I feel so empty!"

"Aw, Ah'm right sorry you're going through all this! Grief isn't nice. But, believe me, it does pass."

"In a million years' time."

"Hey! Even I won't be around then!"

Ellie managed a weary smile at his weak joke, realizing he was trying to ease her discomfort. She changed the subject and asked: "Did you always want to be a soldier? Don't you ever want to have your own place, with your own animals to tend to?"

"Sure. Ah've tried that, back in Kansas with my gran'pa. We worked the land, looked after our animals… Guess Ah'll settle down one day, with a wife and family. But Ah'll have to find me the right woman, first!"

"I wonder what your 'right woman' will look like?" Ellie suggested slyly and with curiosity.

Nathan considered, he gave Ellie a wide grin. "Like you!"

Every time he visited her he brought her food and they shared it between them. Some of the other soldiers had seen his interest in Ellie and they called him 'Injun lover', but Nathan took no notice of them.

He'd already had a fight with one of the young soldiers over Ellie. This was the soldier who had told Nathan to go and fetch the firewood and his name was Bob Perkins.

About four of the soldiers were grouped around the camp fire when Nathan joined them. Bob noticed that Nathan was pouring out a second cup of coffee, and he guessed who this was for. He drawled: "Mighty good of you to help feed the Injun gal – is she worth it?"

Nathan didn't reply, but Bob was a spiteful man. "They say these Injun wimmun ain't virgins – they sleep with anyone!"

There was general course laughter from the men grouped around the fire.

Nathan stopped. He faced Bob. "That's untrue! You're a lewd son of a bitch, Bob!"

Bob carried on riling Nathan. He was jealous of the young man's attraction to Ellie: "Well, you watch your Injun friend, then. It's always the prettiest ones that spread their legs!"

"I won't have you speak 'bout Ellie like that! Injun or not, she's worth ten of you!"

"Hah! Injun lover!" Bob sneered.

Nathan had been about to walk away. He turned and faced his tormentor. "You've called me that once too often!" He growled, and put down the coffee tins.

"Tis true, Injun lover!"

Nathan swung a fist. Bob's head snapped back and he hit the snowy ground with a muted thump. Nathan was on him before he could lift an arm to fend him off.

"Git off me!"

"Ah will – if you apologize f'slangin' Ellie!"

"Tarnation! Ah ain't apologizing!" Bob tried to wriggle free. Nathan still pinned him down, to the amusement of the crowd of soldiers standing around them.

Bob's free hand found some cold snow. He hurled it at Nathan's eyes.

Nathan swore and released his grip as the ice stung his face. Bob was up and at him before Nathan could finish blinking. The two met each other in a brief backbreaking hug, before Bob slashed Nathan's neck with his hand.

Nathan stuck out a foot and tripped Bob over again. The two grappled like heaving bears in the snowy dirt.

"Leave – Ellie – outa – this!" Nathan gasped.

Bob's split mouth contorted into a sneer. He punched Nathan hard, egged on by the now cheering soldiers. The two men slapped and kicked each other, thoroughly provoked with rage in their eyes and dislike in their hearts.

A stern voice boomed at them. "What's a-goin' on here?"

It was Sargent Mallows.

Bob and Nathan broke apart, the crowd of soldiers moving back a little.

"Are you two men fighting? What are you fighting over?"

Nathan jumped to his feet instantly. "Nothing, Sargent!"

Bob, looking a little dazed, slowly got to his feet. "Nothing!" He mumbled, his lip bleeding profusely.

Mallows gave them both a hard stare. "If Capt'n McGinty sees you two fighting like this, he'd order you both t'be chained; don't tempt me t'do that! We've got enough trouble keeping the Injuns apart at times, without you two fighting each other. Get me?"

"Aye, Sargent!"

"Ah'll leave it be this time! But don't you let me ketch you fighting again!"

"Yeah, Sargent!"

Mallows nodded, curtly. "Dismissed! All Company dismissed!" He walked away. Bob glared at Nathan with unforgiving eyes.

"Ah'll git you, Billings!" he'd warned, as Nathan walked stiffly away carrying the now cool coffee.

"Ah'll look out for you, Perkins!" Nathan called back. "It will be *my* pleasure!"

Bob just sneered again and made a fist at Nathan's departing back.

Nathan visited Ellie one evening when it had got warmer and for once, there was no snow on the ground. This was a few weeks after her mother had died, and he brought food again.

Ellie had been sitting far away from the others, distancing herself from her people by camping amongst a grove of Cottonwood trees. She'd built herself a small fire and was staring into this dreamily. She started when she saw Nathan. He smiled at her, his heart warming towards her.

"It isn't much – but cornbread is better than nothing. You must eat."

Because he was thoughtful and seemed to care about her welfare, Ellie tried a mouthful, but found it hard to chew. She spat the bread out.

"Ugh! I can't eat it, Nathan! I don't feel well!"

"You must! You've got to keep going, Ellie!" He crouched down beside her. "Where does it hurt? Maybe Ah can find some herbs for you. Ah know something about them."

Ellie touched her heart. "I've told you before, I am empty, here. I miss Mama." Her eyes began to leak huge, bleak tears. They tumbled down her cheeks, creating brown marks on her dirty earth-streaked face.

In that moment she looked older than she was and Nathan was drawn to hunker down beside her and put his arms around her shoulders, the primitive male responding to the pretty female. She felt his warmth, but it couldn't reach the frozen depths of her soul.

She shrugged him off and stood up abruptly.

Nathan stood too, hands in his overcoat pockets.

"Ah only want to help, Ellie."

"I know. It's just..." she tried to smooth the grazed and torn creases on her deerskin shift, averting her gaze from him, keeping busy with her movements, all attention on her worn out clothes. She was conscious of him standing close to her. In fact, she felt overwhelmed, aware of his masculinity, and she knew that her young body was responding to this.

"I'm too unsettled right now." Yet, at the same time, she wanted to say: 'stay with me.'

"Right, Ah'll be off then. Call me if you need me, Ellie." Nathan bent down to pick up the Winchester rifle he'd leant against a rock. He hesitated. "You're sure you'll be okay?"

She nodded stiffly, standing with her back to him, proud and tense, yet wanting to turn to him, run to him for comfort and scream: Why? Why? Why?

She did start to turn around as he moved, and in that instant, a fierce bellow from the bush alerted both of them. They found themselves confronting a beast from the wilds – a huge black bear, which must have weighed all of 500 lbs. It was padding towards them, now rearing up on its hind legs which were gashed and bleeding. It was moving closer to Ellie than to Nathan.

Ellie screamed, ducking. Nathan swiftly and automatically brought his rifle up to pin-point the lunging creature in his sights, his heart beating rapidly.

The pain-crazed bear surged forward, blowing loudly and snapping its teeth. Nathan fired, the rifle kicking like a crazy mule in his hands.

The bullet missed but diverted the bear from where Ellie was crouching. The bear lumbered back onto all fours, its shaggy fur moving under the powerful muscles of its body. It made off in the direction of the forest. They heard shouts from the main camp, but no one came to investigate the gunfire.

Nathan dropped the rifle as if it was red-hot. He went over to the still-crouching Ellie. "Are you alright?"

"I'm shaking!" Ellie blurted out, tears streaming in earnest down her cheeks again.

She allowed herself to lean against his chunky body, feeling her desire to hug him and not let go. She was glad of his comforting presence, even though the pain of her mother's death still existed. For a moment, she didn't feel so alone.

Nathan patted her gently on the back although he was itching to put his arms around her. "It's alright now; the bear's gone. Poor injured beast. It must have come out of hibernation, still in a daze and walked into a bear trap. Maybe it got away from it somehow! No wonder it was acting crazy! You shouldn't be out here so far from the others, Ellie! I worry about you!"

"Do you?"

Nathan nodded.

"Would you support me, please? I feel a little faint."

Nathan hesitated, taken with a pleasant surprise. "Surely…" He gripped her gently, rocking her to him as if she was a much younger child. He held her head against his chest, wanting this moment to continue for a long time. She felt slender and light in his arms. He said again: "It's alright."

Ellie shook her head, her long hair getting tangled up with the heavy cape around his shoulder. "First, it's Mama dying, and now a Yo-na attack us! I can't take anymore!" She carried on sobbing loudly, although she was too far from the others for them to hear her.

Nathan could think of nothing to say that would offer any comfort, he just held her to him until the storm passed, wishing that he could help her more. She seemed so alone and he liked her a lot, he was beginning to realize that himself.

The little Indian girl, all by herself now, no one to bother about her at the moment… It brought out Nathan's caring side. He realized then that he wasn't a true soldier like the others. He had principles, and one of those principles was not to leave Ellie on her own for too long. He felt protective towards her.

He said, gently: "Ah'm coming back; Ah'm just going to salvage some things for you. You're worn out and you need a decent blanket. Ah'm going to go and get that. Ah know where they keep 'em now! Stay there; Ah'll be back.?"

"… You're definitely coming back?"

"Try an' stop me!"

He wasn't gone long, although, in her misery, Ellie didn't notice. When he did return, he'd brought an almost new, plain blanket with him, and this he wrapped around her where she sat, shivering on the bleak, damp earth.

As he pulled the thick woven cloth around her shoulders Ellie seemed to rouse herself; she reached out and grasped both of his hands, holding them tightly in her own cold ones as if willing some warmth into herself.

"Can you stay with me?"

It was a small, child's voice, afraid of the dark. He thought of the rough companionship of those soldiers whom he slept with, played cards with, joked and smoked with, but this seemed insignificant against the needs of the young Indian girl.

"Alright, but you'd be better off going back to main camp."

"I'd rather stay here – with you."

"Guess ah don't mind."

She sighed and leant against him, not thinking so much about her mother at the moment, but about their lucky escape from the bear, it had jolted her out of her misery a little.

"What would have happened if you hadn't had had that rifle?"

Nathan was practical. "Ah had it; end of story. You're alright, that's the main thing."

"You're bothering a lot about me."

"Ah like you. In fact, Ah can't get you out of my mind!"

Ellie stared wonderingly at him. "I like you, too." She continued to look at him as he leant across and took her face in his hands. She remained still. Nathan bent his head and kissed her gently on the mouth. Ellie tried to move away, unprepared, but his kiss became deeper, longer, and she began to respond, feelings his arms move to her shoulders and tighten around her. It was a long, hard kiss, full of yearning on his part; full of need and loneliness on hers.

Then he let her go. She found she was still trying to clutch hold of him.

"What's the matter?"

Nathan sighed. "You're so young! It's not right! Ah shouldn't touch you!"

She fell silent, fiddling with a lock of her dark hair, not knowing what to say. Instinct found its way for her, she moved her hand and picked up his hand and lifted his arm, placing it around her shoulders. "You said you'd stay with me."

"Ah meant that." He turned and faced her, studying her

thoughtfully. Although she felt exhausted, Ellie smiled wanly.

She picked up his other hand and held it in hers, her dark Indian eyes on him all the time. "Then, stay." she said simply. Then she put her arms around his neck and this time, he didn't argue.

Neither felt the cold as they moved together in a fierce rush making the blanket fall off her shoulders.

They had the privacy, the darkness, and the smoking fire and she wasn't afraid of his man-ness.

No one heard their whispers of love in the dark night as it closed above them. Somewhere, an owl hooted, but they didn't hear it, lost as they were to each other's needs.

Love came quickly the first time. They moved together like two young, lissome lion cubs, pawing each other. Eventually, the tempo waned and slowed, he held her to him, his breathing a little heavy. She relaxed against his taut body. They spoke little that first time. Later, as the moon arose high in the sky, he pulled her to him again and held her carefully, as if she were Dresden china. When they moved together a second time, it was slow and deliberate and very lovely. A time of beauty and wonder of being together as they entwined, holding, breathing, making the rhythm of love something other than a special gift to each other...

Towards the morning he said to her: "Ah'm glad I stayed with you."

Ellie didn't answer. She was fast asleep.

Later, in the morning they had time to talk shortly to each other.

"I know you're in the army but why did you volunteer for this cold walk? Wouldn't you rather be back at home living with your gran'pa?" Ellie asked Nathan as they prepared to rise.

"Well... Ah'm a bit of a traveler, I guess. I can bivouac in hot or cold areas. Besides, you don't know it yet, but where we're headed, it will be a better place for you, Ellie."

"You really say so?"

"Ah know so. That's why Ah'm here, because Ah care for you, an' Ah want to help you on your way." He took her cold hand in his warm one. "We can travel on together, eh?"

"I'd like that; yes."

Nathan helped her get ready for the walk. She was very exhausted and, in her mind, she carried the charred memory of her mother's death, deeply embedded in her heart. So deeply, that it was then that Ellie herself fell ill and became sick with the weary passage, with just that one evening of love to soften the journey.

She had developed a bad cough.

It all happened so quickly. She began to falter in the next few weeks, feeling weary and light-headed. Her breathing became shallow and she developed an intermittent fever. Her chest hurt her at times as well. She became so sick that she was even unable to cry, or speak properly to Nathan, and she wondered why she felt like this.

It was the women who could have told her. It was in the eyes.

Chapter Thirteen

The Wolf and the Raven

After several weeks of more walking, Ellie began feeling sick, and her cough got worse. She found it hard to breathe and just managed to tag along with the others. There was a sharp pain at the base of her spine as well as the pain in her chest.

She spoke to Najun briefly, about her ailments. He told her to rest as much as she could, and he would see if there were any spaces in the wagons for her. It was her cough that worried him more than her sickness. He went off to find Clara to ask her to keep an eye on the suffering girl.

Ellie was glad when McGinty bought the Indians straggling groups to the outskirts of a small township, where they could barter for food and tobacco, and have a well-earned rest.

For one night only McGinty left Sergeant Mallows in charge and rode back into the town. He figured that after months in the saddle he was entitled to a proper bath, and a drink. So he made for the town's saloon.

It was a small saloon, a little run-down, but the whisky was good and he drank it neat.

Then he asked for a room and a bath and got one. Moments later, standing in his under-vest and pants, his gun holster slung onto the nearest chair, he heard a knock at his door. "Come in!"

A blond woman entered the room. She was pert and pretty with an elfin-shaped face and wide, wide hips. She was dressed in the style of a whore – low bodice, tight, calf-length flared skirt with calf-high boots. She was carrying a jug.

"Hi, there! I'm Suzy Sunshine! Who be you?"

McGinty told her his name and rank. She nodded. She was busy pouring hot water into his tub.

"Mind if I stay with you? I figured you might need some

company!"

McGinty wasn't adverse to this idea. "Ah don't mind if you don't, Ma'am!"

"Uh, call me Suzy!"

"Okay – Suzy!"

"I could do with a drink, though!"

McGinty inclined his head towards the door. "Feel free! Ah won't run away!"

"Okay, sugar!" She gave a soft laugh. "I'll be back now!"

McGinty took off the remainder of his clothes and sank into the hot bath, relaxing in its warmth.

Suzy Sunshine returned with a whiskey bottle and a couple of cigars. She lit one and placed it in McGinty's mouth. "Like me to rub you down?"

"Guess Ah don't mind!"

She giggled. "My! I like a man with a hairy chest!"

McGinty grabbed her soapy, wandering hand. "Do you figure on staying?"

"For a sum, mister!" She named what she had in mind.

McGinty nodded. "Rub me down, Susy Sunshine!" he ordered. "Then – bed!"

Suzy said: "I like to be ordered about, so be real mean to me, won't you?" She was already taking off the first layer of her bodice.

McGinty grinned, feeling the strain of the walk fall away from his shoulders...

He might have stayed a little longer than he'd intended to. Suzy was a good bedfellow and she was in awe of him when she learnt that he was leading the Indians to a new territory. She dubbed him 'Indian Saint' which was a little far from the truth. McGinty was no saint.

He'd told her a little about some of the Indians he was escorting. He mentioned Ellie.

"There's this Injun gal – real pretty – she has the spirit o' a man! Always harassing me! Always getting' in my way! Whatever I do or says to her she just bounces right back!"

Suzy laughed. She snuggled up to him. "Sounds like she's the reason you've been driven into my arms!"

"Not really, Ah guess. Ah just want to get her out of my system!"

"Are you sure you're not shining a torch for her?"

"Heaven forbid! She's only fifteen! She's just a gal – a danged bewitching gal!"

"So you do fancy her?"

"Ah haven't got feelings either way! She's just a darn nuisance!"

"Then I think you admire her."

McGinty took a deep breath. He said, to his surprise: "Mebbe Ah do! You could be right about it. Ah just hadn't seen her in an admiring light!"

Suzy laughed again. "Sounds like you don't understand women! This gal just has a lot of spirit, that's all – like me!"

McGinty turned to her. He took her pointed face in his hands. "Then Ah think it's time Ah found some o' that spirit of yours!"

She said: "Give me a good solid kiss then soldier, otherwise, you're wasting my time!"

"Alright, Lady – let me show you what a good solid kiss should be like!"

"An' don't tickle me with your moustache!"

He rolled onto her. For a while the bedsprings creaked and groaned.

Later, he said his goodbyes to her like a gentlemen and returned to camp, glad of her sunshine, but still surprised that it had taken a woman to point out to him the fact that he admired Ellie Sheldon Starr. He'd never ever before admired an Indian!

<> <> <>

When they left town, some of the younger Cherokee and Choctaw Indians, who were less tired than the rest of the tribe, were allowed to hunt with the soldiers after winter buffalo, a small herd that was roaming nearby. Most of the soldiers had got used to the Indians by this time, and some of them had become kinder to the suffering tribes. They were so far from home now that it wasn't worth it for the Indians to try and get away from the camp.

Ordinarily, it was the medicine man that would have been consulted as to the most propitious time to hunt buffalo, but the soldiers did it their way; McGinty grouped the wagons into tight circles and the soldiers rode out on their fastest ponies with fire-power in their pockets. The Indians were given ponies too, but were not allowed weapons. They joined in the hunt as best they could seeing the soldiers shoot the young bulls. They were considered a tastier meal than the old bulls. It was not the Indian way to shoot buffalo, for these people would have shot arrows into the flank between the lower ribs and the hip and made sure the beast died with dignity. The soldiers just shot and left the buffalo to die of their gunshot wounds, whilst the Indians and the chopper men later went around in groups and cut them up.

The snow-covered ground soon lay littered with dead beasts. But the Indians had enjoyed the headlong ride as they dashed beside the young bulls and turned them into the path of a bullet. It was like being home again. Eagerly, they skinned the bison of the parts that they used and needed, and, secretly, in their hearts, they gave thanks for this rich surplus of meat.

It was the women who processed the bison meat and skin; the flesh was sliced into strips and dried on poles over slow fires to make pemmican.

For a little while in camp that night, there was an air of gaiety about the men, including the dour soldiers, who were happy with the hunt. But Ellie didn't notice. She was sitting with the women, feeling feverish and heavy-eyed, with no energy. Clara and Nancy noticed and made her lie down beside the camp fire, where she instantly fell asleep.

The next morning she awoke beside the dead, charred fire with a dreadful, low, intense, throbbing back pain.

Suddenly, she got up, disappeared behind a straggling thorn bush and was sick. When she came back, glassy-eyed, she found Clara and Nancy beside her.

The pair looked at each other knowingly.

Clara said roughly: "Sit, child! Rest here!" She produced from her medicine bundle which, like her husband Najun, she always carried around with her, a small shawl, beautifully crocheted with woven Indian beads. She spread the garment on the ground and practically pushed Ellie down onto it.

Nancy grabbed hold of Ellie's cold hand. She asked earnestly: "What is wrong, sister?"

"I have been sick. That cornbread—"

Clara still spoke roughly: "It isn't the cornbread, child. When was your last moontime?"

"I – I can't remember!"

Nancy pressed Ellie's hand. "It was at the second last full moon! I remember because I did not feel very good either!"

Ellie shrugged and Nancy persisted: "That was eight weeks ago, Ellie. You seem to be very, very late if you don't mind me saying so!"

Ellie shivered, trying to frame a question that wouldn't come through her cracked, cold, stiff lips: "What are you trying to say?" She coughed, harshly.

Nancy shrugged. "Work it out. You've had a bad tummy since last week."

At that moment, Nathan walked by the group, ready to put a hand up to give the Indian girl a special wave, but his hand stayed in mid-air when he saw the mute, frozen, stunned expression on her young face.

Wondering what was amiss, he wandered over. Ellie saw him

coming and instantly got to her feet and ran away.

Astonished, Nathan stared after her, and then looked at the Indian women.

Their faces stared stonily back at him. Uncomfortably, he rang his finger around his collar, then shrugged and walked away, trying to see where Ellie had run off to. He couldn't find her... But someone else did.

The woods was Ellie's refuge. She somehow had found the energy to spurt through the tangled undergrowth, diving through the twigs and clumps of melting snow and managing, in her headlong flight, to scratch her face badly. It was only when a hacking cough stopped her from going further that she stilled, leaning on a tree branch for support, her heart thudding, feeling washed-out and fearful.

Were Clara and Nancy right? Was she pregnant?

She was unaware that in her sudden surge into the forest that she had attracted the attention of a soldier, a sentry on guard duty, who was none other than Bob Perkins. He'd noticed her swift exit into the forest and had decided that this was his day for enjoying what life offered...

Bob sighed: "Shouldn't be a-goin' that-a-way, darling," he said softly, to himself. With a grin, he set down his rifle, hoisted himself up from the dank earth and followed the Indian girl.

The strong trunk of a tree supported her young body for a moment whilst Ellie tried to get her breath back. Behind her, she heard the snap of a twig and glanced around sharply, but could see nothing.

It was gloomy in the forest. She realized that she shouldn't have come in here unprotected. But she did not feel afraid at that moment.

She went to move and a hand caught her wrist. She whirled round recognizing Bob who were always on guard in the night and in the early part of the morning.

"What you doin' here, beauty! No place f' a litt'lin like you!"

Ellie tried to shake her hand loose, but it was held tightly:

"Let go! Go away! Can't I have some privacy?"

"Sure. But Ah'll stop wich ya', Ah guess! Come here!"

Bob pulled her towards him, trying to drag her down on the dirt floor.

Realizing the danger, Ellie struggled, suddenly regaining her strength, her back pain and fatigue forgotten in the surge of adrenalin that shook her body. Bob somehow managed to pull her to the ground and get on top of her. "Quit strugglin' Injun!" He pinned her arms whilst she tried to pin her legs together. She felt his hand heavy on her small breast, pulling, tugging, and tearing at her clothes and his hot mouth on her lips.

She struggled like a wildcat, kicked, pulled, got her arms and legs free and managed to lash out with her elbows and hands, trying to bite and screamed shrilly. No one heard. The camp hadn't woken up yet. And if any soldier caught her muffled cries for help, they weren't interfering.

Something heard. Call it a protective guardian, or maybe, the raven that flew to the branch above her head arrived there as a curious onlooker. Whatever it was, this messenger gave her strength and initiative. She used it, struggling under the soldier's weight like a weaving snake.

"Get – off – me! Someone's watching!"

Bob relaxed his grip a moment. "Eh?"

Her leg swung out, hit the soldier in the groin and he rolled sideways with a startled, winded grunt. Spurred on, Ellie rolled on her tummy, clawing her way into a sitting position, then to a standing one. She turned to run, feeling suddenly weak-kneed – only to come face to face with a wolf. It was another frightening thing to happen to her; to be so close to this creature. She couldn't stop the shriek. But although the wolf put his ears back, he regarded her steadily with alert, knowing eyes.

The shock of seeing the animal so close made her stand still.

Uncannily, she and the wolf surveyed each other for several

heartbeats. The wolf did not look menacing. He had clumps of fur missing from his wiry body and Ellie was very sure that it was the same animal that she'd christened 'Ghost' whom she'd seen following the camp on more than one occasion. But how had he got here? She'd last seen the creature the other side of the Mississippi?

Then she forgot about the wolf as she bent over in sudden pain, a cry of anguish escaping from her throat, twisting to the ground before she could stop herself.

Behind her, Bob was picking himself up, moaning and swearing, weaving purposely towards her again. She was unable to move. In her despair her heartbeats of fear suffocated her and she felt as if she was going to faint.

Although a wolf doesn't normally attack a man, seeing the moving, threatening figure behind Ellie the animal gave the soldier a fixed, aggressive stare, assumed a high body posture and raised his hackles, emitting a low growl. Drawing back its ears it jumped onto the soldier, pinning him to the ground, giving Ellie the chance to escape. Ellie took that chance. Clutching at bushes and tree branches, bent almost double, and perspiring with her efforts she managed to make some progress – putting as much space as she could from her attacker, who had screamed out when the wolf sprung on him.

The raven flew to the branch Ellie was holding onto and it seemed to be saying: "Follow me! I'm with you!"

Ellie looked back. Bob was rolling on the ground with the wolf hindering him from getting up, worrying at his arm, his paws slammed against his chest, pinning him to the ground.

Somehow, Ellie crawled away, hearing the soldier call out for help, trying to get her senses right and head back to the camp, but it felt like she was being held in liquid syrup. So difficult it was to move her heavy limbs, but she knew she had to get away. She managed to stand up, grabbing onto tree branches to steady her shaking body.

Again, it was uncanny, but at each branch she stumbled towards it seemed as if the raven was already there before her, leading her on, offering its winged guidance. It was so close to her at one stage that she could almost have lifted a hand and touched the bird's head.

Somehow, she stumbled back into the camp, coughing badly and trying to adjust her torn clothing, just as the medicine woman Clara came towards her, an anxious look on her face.

Clara called out: "Martha! Nancy!" then offered her arms and her support to the ravaged child who tottered towards her, eyes glazed and stricken, for she was losing the baby so early and the medicine woman knew this...

Chapter Fourteen

Ellie

Somehow, Clara had found her a space within one of the store wagons. Here she made Ellie rest and she was only too glad to do so. She dreamed a lot, in a semi-conscious pain-filled daze, unaware that she was losing the baby or that she'd gained an infection that Clara had not the means to treat properly for they had no more cramp bark.

By then she was in a stupor, unable to judge time or space, so deep was her pain, her exhaustion, and her will to carry on…

The Indian woman let a guilty, concerned Nathan visit her. Clara had told him about the intended rape and Nathan was all for hunting Bob Perkins down, calling him a "Cussed low-sprung Jackal! Wait till Ah get my hands on him! Ah'll get him!"

But, first, he insisted on seeing Ellie alone. He held her slender hand in his chunky one, cradling it to his face and rubbing it against his lips in an effort to rouse her from her stupor.

"ELLIE! O' my lovely, for God's sakes, speak to me!"

There were genuine tears in his brown eyes. He really loved the little Indian girl. It hadn't just been a passing fancy. She stirred, slightly, and he pressed her cold hand harder, stroking her taut, wan face at the same time.

"Wake up, Ellie! It's me – Nathan! Speak t'me – tell me you're going to get better – *Please!*"

She made no answer. Her eyes were closed and heavy-lidded, her olive skin pale and her pinched lips almost blue-grey with the cold. He couldn't bear to see her like this.

In desperation, he shook her shoulders. At this fierce movement her eyes briefly fluttered open. There was no expression in them; she seemed as if locked in a tomb, a timeless body of life, breathing shallowly in a half world of light and shadow.

Frightened by the empty look in her eyes, Nathan shook her harder.

"Ellie!" He moaned. *"Stay with me!"*

She still made no movement, no sound, and he sank back on his haunches with his eyes covered, weeping.

Then a light touch on his hand made him uncover his eyes, dazedly.

She was awake!

"Ellie!" He bent forward, taking hold of her hand again, crushing it to his chest. "Talk to me! Can't you? Can't you say anything?"

She swallowed, her eyes on his face, and then swallowed again. She mimed drinking. He understood that she wanted water. He almost fell out of the wagon in his haste to get her what she needed.

Clara ran towards him. "Water – quickly!" Nathan sprang back into the dark wagon and grabbed hold of Ellie's hand again.

Feeling his touch, she opened her eyes. There was a little more life in them now – but barely.

"Nathan…" It was nothing more than a slow drawl. "I-I'm hurting!"

He found that his own throat was dry. "Ah know. We're doing the best we can for you, Ellie. Your medicine man is finding herbs. His woman is here if you want to talk to her!"

Ellie coughed harshly, holding her stomach and slowly shook her head. It was agonizing for him to watch her cough so badly. She seemed to bring up a greenish mucous that had him further worried at her deterioration.

"What's that stuff you're bringing up, Ellie? Ah don't like it!"

Ellie coughed again. She couldn't answer him, just tried to sweep away her long dark hair with a weak hand. It lay tangled in wild swathes against the white sack of grain they had laid her back onto.

She said, drowsily. "I only want...you...with...me! The baby..."

He wasn't sure he'd heard her right. "Did you say baby? What do you mean? What baby?!"

Her eyes flickered sideways at him. "They...have'nt...told you? I...am pregnant!"

"O, Lord!"

He grasped her hand tighter. "Ellie – Ah'm sorry – No! Ah mean, Ah'm pleased, but you must rest if you're pregnant! Listen, Ah kin ride out; get a doc to come to you. There's another town we're heading for, only a few miles away!"

Ellie groaned, closed her eyes. She forced herself to say, haltingly: "I...love...you, Nathan!"

He was in too much of a rush to respond, his mind on more urgent things. "Ah'll go get my horse."

Fired with enthusiasm for this idea he prepared to go backwards out of the wagon, completely forgetting his need to fight with Bob Perkins, but Ellie somehow found the strength to grip his hand this time and her hold stopped him.

"I'm frightened. What...is happening...to me, Nathan? The pain is bad! I'm...bleeding!"

He stared down at her seriously as she squirmed and grimaced in pain. Frowning, he called out to Najun's wife as he knew her title: "Clara!"

Alerted by her name, Clara swiftly entered the wagon. She took one look at the agonized expression on Ellie's face and whirled on Nathan.

"You!" There was scorn in her voice. "I should never have let you see her! You've done enough harm!"

Nathan ignored her defiant, unfriendly stance. "Maybe Ah done wrong, but Ah was going to get help for her. Ah can take a horse – get the doc... "

Clara relented a little. "That sounds a better idea. Alright, soldier! Find yourself a horse and ride hard!"

Nathan needed no second bidding. He was out of the wagon and running for his horse as fast as he could, leaving Clara to to strip off her petticoat to staunch the blood that Ellie was losing…

Nathan had already saddled his horse in readiness for the next march. He swung into the saddle, hearing one of the soldiers shout out: "Hey – Nathan! Doggone it, Nathan – hey!"

But Nathan was gone.

One of the soldiers ran to McGinty who was checking food supplies. "Man away, sir!"

"Eh? Who?"

"Nathan Billings, sir!"

Dang the boy! McGinty knew the Indian girl, Ellie, was in a bad way. He thought he knew why Nathan was riding out. He strode quickly towards the trundling wagon that Ellie had been laid out in.

He was stopped by Martha before he reached it. She calmly stepped down from the wagon and stood directly in McGinty's path, her chin held high, her arms solidly folded. "That's far enough! We've a sick girl here. She doesn't want to talk to you!"

McGinty drew up short. He surveyed the older woman thoughtfully. "Where's he gone?"

She knew who he meant. "To town. To get a doctor."

"I didn't authorize it."

Martha drew a sharp breath. "You wouldn't have allowed it."

McGinty considered the truth coldly. He nodded slowly.

"How bad is Ellie?"

"Plenty bad."

"It's never been my policy to wet-nurse the sick – even Ellie. Ah can't wait for a doctor. We're moving out as soon as Ah have the food list done, so get ready."

Martha glared at him. "*She's losing a baby you inconsiderate son of a bitch!* You want that on your conscience? Moving out will kill her!"

"Look – I've lost me a soldier, thanks to her misbehaving!"

Martha nearly exploded with indignation. "Well – what about me – I've lost me nearly all my family!" she said. "And a lot of it's been through you!" She added, tersely: "If this girl dies, so help me, *I'll kill you!*"

McGinty sneered. "Ah'm not wasting time wich'ya. Ah'm going after the boy!"

Martha heard him call for his horse.

"The young fool! Ah'll not have this happening on my patch without my permission!" McGinty swore as he vaulted his horse. Aloud, to one of his men, he snapped: "Wait for me! Ah'll be back!"

Using the reins as a whip, he slapped the horse on both sides of its slender neck and dug in his knees. "Ya! Giddup there!" They shot like a cannon gun straight out of the camp, McGinty holding on grimly to his excited horse.

Martha compressed her lips, and went to rejoin her grandchild in the wagon.

Clara was gatheringmore petticoats from the other women. They'd run out of bandages. Martha took Ellie's hand in her own rough ones, murmuring: "My grandchild, my only grandchild... Come back to us! I'll be here for you! Let me tell you stories like I used to do in the past, when we lived happily in Ahoama!"

There was no answer. Ellie was deeply asleep. The older woman raised her weary eyes to Clara, who could only shake her head, looking troubled.

"What have I done to deserve this?" Martha asked. Her aged voice cracked as if her throat had closed up. She added tiredly. "There is nothing left for me here, if she dies..."

Clara crunched her eyebrows together: "Don't say that! There is still hope, Martha."

"Hope, yes. But I am thinking there is still something I can do for Ellie... I wish I knew what it was... Oh, yes! Now I know what I can do for her! I can do it for everyone!"

"What's that? You're not talking any sense!"

Martha glanced at her. A wild light shone from her aged eyes, and she beheld Clara with a look of tenderness. "You will hear about it!" she said, obliquely.

Clara still looked mystified as Martha again left the wagon.

No one was guarding the horses.

Ellie had relapsed back into a light coma despite the pain. She was very weak. She dreamed heavily. In this twilight state between the living and the dead, the left brain and the right brain co-existing together, she became psychic and prophetic and saw cloud-like shapes forming into faces. In her dream she saw a bridge. Where she stood there was darkness around her, but on the other side of the bridge there was bright light. As one such face formed in the light she saw it was her grandfather, old Chief Jacob Whiteleaf. In her worn-out stupor he spoke to her: "Child, enter the temple; come to me… I will show you the way. There is light coming – much light. It will dazzle you, but you will not be alone any longer. We are all here, waiting for you. You will find your way to us…"

Then she even saw the face of her cousin, Jobe, as well as her mother. They both seemed to smile down at her, saying nothing, yet their eyes spelt warmth and understanding. Alison's cold eyes that had seemed so distant were no longer full of ice, but full of love, and Ellie thought she could discern real happiness behind the mask on her mother's face.

She was unaware that she was entering her own dreamland, slipping away from physical reality like rainwater soaking into dry sand.

In this stricken, surreal daze, Ellie began to see a road ahead of her. It looked wide and true, strong and straight. Well into her warming dream where there was no pain, she followed that road, listening to the old chieftain, and as she followed it so he appeared to guide her on, with the raven of the woods following her as well, flying above her shoulder. She seemed somehow to leave the weary clan of Indians behind, that poor sodden bunch of humankind, chained forever to their stony trail, following their wagons and the horses. She left the bad track...

Alerted again by the girl's shallow breathing and her silence, Clara stopped trying to stem the flow of blood. She placed a rough hand on Ellie's forehead in sudden concern and understanding. Her husband, Najun came and stood at the wagon's entrance with the herbs he had found clutched tightly in his hand.

His woman looked at him, her face a mask of worry. Then her eyes slid back to Ellie.

In her head, Ellie was following her own trail. She knew she had stumbled upon something totally stupendous, totally unique, although she didn't know it herself... For as her spirit left her body her world had begun to change. No longer was the ground stony and cold, instead it had begun to get warmer, sand trickling down from the rocks from where she traveled. As she passed them with a ghostly Nathan, now solicitously carrying her limp form, she managed to open her eyes and notice that the icy rivers were now no more; instead there were blue rivers, full of jostling, bouncy water, and fat trout jumping in the shallow streams. She could see and hear the birds whistling and singing to each other in the branches of the trees and her heart began, beat by beat, to warm up again.

The whole scenery had changed to blue skies and bright dawns, where marvelous colors of light swept like a painter's brush across the sky.

She could see it all – a harvest of colored blossom streaking through the skies, like a glowing fireball.

She turned to Nathan, emerging from her trance for a moment. "Where are we?"

He just smiled, his square, rustic face creasing into a giant grin of happiness that she was at last noticing her new surroundings.

"You're home, Ellie." he said, simply. And that was all he needed to say.

For the first time in many long months, hearing his words, she felt hope.

Her mother may have gone, seen briefly in a distant haze, but Nathan was here with her, and everything – *everything* – seemed to be returning.

She felt she had come full circle and that her walk – that trail of tears – was over...

<> <> <>

Riding hell for leather over a windswept, rugged hill, Nathan suddenly brought his horse to an abrupt standstill. A bullet had just whizzed past his ear.

Snow was falling again, bleak and bleary and he felt the harsh whine of a strong breeze tear at his ear-length hair, caressing the whiskers on his cheek.

He turned his head and saw another rider on the horizon, moving fast towards him.

Nathan was debating whether to canter on when the rider, nearer now, called out: "Stop right there, boy!"

He recognized McGinty's voice.

Nathan shouted: "You shot at me! Why are you throwing all that lead around?"

"Ah was trying to stop you." McGinty finally drew level with him. He blew out his cheeks and asked: "Are you quitting?"

"You know Ah'm not! Ah'm going to get help for Ellie."

'The Injun gal!" McGinty sneered.

"Ah love her!"

"Love – hah! A fool's dream, boy! Ah can't have a dratted hold-up like this! We have to get back and get moving!"

"Ah'm not coming back with you yet. Ah'm getting the doc for her!"

For answer, McGinty cocked his gun and leveled it at Nathan's burly chest.

"You're not going to do anything, boy! Ah'm danged if Ah—"

They both heard the gun shot that came out of nowhere. McGinty's chin dropped to his chest in disbelief.

Blood suddenly blossomed upon his army coat. He fell from his horse and crumpled to the ground, a look of complete surprise on his face.

Nathan whirled round, blinking rapidly because the snow got in his eyes. His own hand had gone for his Winchester.

Sitting majestically on a horse she'd stolen from the soldier's ranks, Martha slowly lowered her smoking rifle.

"I said I'd kill him if Ellie died."

Nathan blinked at her, trying to register the words. "Is she... Did you say 'died'? Is Ellie dead? Oh no! Not my Ellie!"

To Nathan's surprise, Martha slid slowly from her horse's saddle. "Yes. She's dead; I have lost my granddaughter." She let go of the pommel and sank suddenly to her knees, as if her aged body could no longer carry her heavy weight. She threw her arms high and opened her mouth wide, letting out a long eerie screech full of rage, pain and suffering, the tears she'd held back now gushing like a waterfall down her deeply furrowed face. The hairs on the back of Nathan's neck stood on end as the sound of the scream echoed around him in the empty snow.

He wanted to go over to her and help her up, but he couldn't move. He was stunned at Ellie's death. Although he knew in his heart that she'd been ill, he couldn't accept that she had died. Not yet.

Nathan closed his eyes, feeling the cold on his eyelids.

In his mind he heard Ellie's voice on the wind.

"Nathan! Goodbye Nathan! I love you!"

On impulse, his hand went for his rifle. He didn't know what he intended doing, except that he intended something.

"No! That isn't the way!" Martha had moved closer to Nathan.

He hadn't heard her. So fixed was he on his own sorrow. Now she grabbed his hand with her cold hand and clasped it tightly. "You are a good man – a good soldier. But you must overcome this!"

He lowered his face to the horse's warm neck. He knew there was no need to go on, to get help for Ellie. It was over. All at once he felt very lonely. He sobbed.

After a long while the wind blew away his tears. As they dried on his cheek he stared down at the impassive Indian woman.

"You just killed my captain…?"

"He wanted to move us on – like he is always doing. He wouldn't stop to help Ellie… I was losing her like I've lost the others. I couldn't allow that anymore… When I saw him ride after you something snapped inside me. I knew I had to stop him… I suppose he is dead?"

Nathan raised an eyebrow. He leapt off his horse and bent down beside the huddled figure of his captain and tried for a pulse. McGinty's thin mouth gaped slightly, his sightless green eyes were open to the ominous storm-ridden sky, and his fair hair blew in the wind. "Yep. He's a goner – he'll be giving us no more orders."

As he stood, he said heavily, to Martha: "Ah understand your grief over losing Ellie. It's mine now, too. God, but Ah loved her!"

"I know that. But, you are young; you will heal. But my grief hasn't had time to – it is raw. I have lost so many in such a short time."

"Ah guess so… What about our baby?"

Martha shook her head. She said sorrowfully. "Ellie miscarried."

"Yeah. Ah realized that when Ah left her. Ah couldn't do anything about it – although Ah wanted to. But, did the baby kill her?"

"No. Ellie died of hunger and pneumonia and her personal

loss. The baby – your baby – did not stand a good chance because of Ellie's state of health. I'm sorry."

"Ah'm sorry, too. She was a lovely gal – full o' spirit!"

"Yes. I shall remember her that way – courageous and determined, with fire in her eyes! Not as she became – low and crushed by the cough she had. It was the pneumonia that got her in the end. She didn't have the strength to fight her miscarriage."

Nathan felt that he had to say it again. "Ah'm so sorry – for her, for the baby, for you, an' for me." He was crying again.

"Then, you'll understand why I had to kill the captain?"

Nathan nodded. "Ah should have done the same!" he said, fiercely. "But Ah was a coward!"

Martha shook her head again. "You were willing to risk everything for Ellie; you are no coward!"

But Nathan was thinking of other things. "Would he have shot me for deserting?"

Martha nodded.

Nathan said: "Then Ah thank you. Wado!" He rubbed heavily at his eyes.

Martha nodded again. She said: "What will you do now?"

He thought. There was no need to go back to the camp. After all, with Ellie gone, there was nothing to go back for. He realized he'd had a belly-full of the army. It meant nothing to him anymore. "Guess Ah'll take French leave an' head home to Kansas. Do you want to come with me? They'll arrest you and hang you for shooting the captain. You know that, don't you?"

"I am not afraid of death. There are those who escaped to the mountains. I would track them and join them again, but I would not go far – I am too old."

"But you'd be with your kind."

"Yes. I would be with my kind... You must make good speed from here, before they send scouts to find us both! You yourself are in danger because they'll think you shot Yellow Beard!"

"Ah will." Nathan remounted his horse and turned him

eastwards, his eyes still misty with tears.

He glanced down at the old Indian woman. "Ah thought the world o' Ellie—" His voice broke.

Martha looked fierce for a moment, then, she nodded. "You are not at fault; you gave her care and consolation whilst she lived. My eyes see this. So, remember that! May your God go with you! Farewell, my White friend!"

Nathan nodded grimly and raised his hand to her: "An' may yours go with you! Farewell!"

Nathan spurred forward into the endless snow. With guilt and grief as his companions, he headed home to his county. It was a mighty long way, but he had a lifetime to get there. And he had a lot of hiding to do.

THE END

**TOP HAT
BOOKS**

Historical fiction that lives.

We publish fiction that captures the contrasts, the achievements, the optimism and the radicalism of ordinary and extraordinary times across the world.

We're open to all time periods and we strive to go beyond the narrow, foggy slums of Victorian London. Where are the tales of the people of fifteenth century Australasia? The stories of eighth century India? The voices from Africa, Arabia, cities and forests, deserts and towns? Our books thrill, excite, delight and inspire.

The genres will be broad but clear. Whether we're publishing romance, thrillers, crime, or something else entirely, the unifying themes are timescale and enthusiasm. These books will be a celebration of the chaotic power of the human spirit in difficult times. The reader, when they finish, will snap the book closed with a satisfied smile.